Fear of Dying

Fear
of
Dying

Erica
Jong

CANONGATE
Edinburgh · London

Published in Great Britain in 2015 by Canongate Books Ltd,
14 High Street, Edinburgh EH1 1TE

www.canongate.tv

1

First published in the United States in 2015 by St. Martin's Press,
175 Fifth Avenue, New York, N.Y. 10010. www.stmartins.com

ISBN 978 1 78211 743 8
Export ISBN 978 1 78211 744 5

Designed by Kelly S. Too

Printed and bound in Great Britain by Clays Ltd, St Ives plc

MIX
Paper from
responsible sources
FSC
www.fsc.org   FSC® C018072

For my BFF, Gerri
&
L'Ultimo Marito, Ken

Days pass and the years vanish, and we walk sightless among miracles. Lord, fill our eyes with seeing and our minds with knowing; Let there be moments when Your Presence, like lightning, illumines the darkness in which we walk. Help us to see, wherever we gaze, that the bush burns unconsumed. And we, clay touched by God, will reach out for holiness, and exclaim in wonder, "How filled with awe is this place and we did not know it!"

—Attributed to *Mishkan Tefilah: A Reform Siddur*

Fear of Dying

PART I

Fall

1

Happily Married Woman, or
Is There Sex After Death?

I generally avoid temptation *unless I can't resist it.*

——Mae West (stealing from Oscar Wilde)

I used to love the power I had over men. Walking down the street, my mandolin-shaped ass swaying and swinging to their backward eyes. How strange that I only completely knew this power when it was gone—or transferred to my daughter, all male eyes on her nubile twentyish body, promising babies. I missed this power. It seemed that the things that had come to replace it—marriage, maternity, the wisdom of the mature woman (ugh, I hate that phrase)—weren't worth the candle. Ah, the candle! Standing up. Burning for me. Full of sound and fury signifying everything. I know I should fade away like a good old girl and spare my daughter the embarrassments of my passions, but I can't any more than I can conveniently die. Life is passion. But now I know what passion costs, so it's hard to be quite so carefree anymore.

But was I ever carefree? Was anyone? Wasn't love always an exploding cigar? Didn't Gypsy Rose Lee say, "God is love, but get it in writing"? And didn't Fanny Brice say, "Love is like a card trick—once you know how it works, it's no fun anymore"?

Those old broads knew a thing or two. And did they give up? Never!

I'm not going to tell you—yet—how old I am or how many times I've been married. (I have decided never to get any older than fifty.) My husband and I read the obituaries together more often than we have sex. I'm only going to say that when all the troubles of my family of origin engulfed me and I realized that my marriage could not save me, I reached a point where I was just unhinged enough to put the following ad on Zipless.com, a sex site on the Internet:

> Happily married woman with extra erotic energy seeks happily married man to share same. Come celebrate Eros one afternoon per week. Discretion guaranteed by playful, pretty, imaginative, witty woman. Send e-mail and recent picture. New York area.

Talk about a woman on the verge of a nervous breakdown! It was autumn in New York—season of mellow mists, Jewish holidays, and five-thousand-dollar-a-plate benefits for chic diseases. A time of new beginnings (Yom Kippur), starting over (Rosh Hashanah), and laying in acorns against a barren winter (Succoth). When I placed the ad, I had thought of myself as a sophisticate coolly interviewing lovers. But now I was suddenly overcome with panic. I began fantasizing about what sort of creeps, losers, retreads, extortionists, and homicidal maniacs such an ad would attract—and then I got so busy with calls from my ailing parents and pregnant daughter that I forgot all about it.

A few minutes went by. Then suddenly the responses poured out of the Internet like coins out of a slot machine.

I was almost afraid to look. After a couple of beats, I couldn't resist. It was like hoping I had won the lottery. The first response showed a scanned Polaroid of an erect penis—a tawny uncircumcised specimen with a drop of dew winking at the tip. Under the photo, on the white border, was scrawled: "Without Viagra." The accompanying e-mail was concise:

> I like your style. Have always risen for assertive women.
> Send nude shot and measurements.

The next one began like this:

> Dear Seeker,
>   Sometimes we think it's carnality we want when actually we long for Jesus. We discover that if we open our hearts and let Him in, all sorts of satisfaction undreamt of can be ours. Perhaps you think you are seeking Eros, but Thanatos is what you really seek. In Jesus, there is eternal life. He is the lover who never disappoints, the friend who is loyal forever. It would be an honor to meet and counsel you . . .

A telephone number was proffered: 1-800-JESUS-4U.

I threw all the responses in the virtual garbage can, deleted them, and shut down the computer. I must have been insane to give an authentic e-mail address. That was the end of it, I thought, deluding myself. Another bad idea aborted. I went about my wifelife like an automaton. I had always been impulsive, and impulsive people know how to back away from their impulses. Sex was trouble—at any age. But by sixty—oops, I gave it away—it was a joke. Women were not allowed

to have passion at sixty. We were supposed to become grandmothers and retreat into serene sexlessness. Sex was for
twenty, thirty, forty, even fifty. Sex at sixty was an embar-
rassment. Even if you still looked good, you *knew* too much.
You knew all the things that could go wrong, all the cons you
could set yourself up for, all the dangers of playing with strangers. You knew discretion was a dream. And now my e-mail
was out there for all the crazy phishers and pishers!

Besides, I adored my husband, and the last thing I wanted
to do was hurt him. I had always known that marrying someone twenty years older put me at risk for spending my sunset
years without sex. But he had given me so much else. I'd married him when I was forty-five and he was sixty-five and we'd
had a great ride together. He had healed all the old wounds
of my earlier marriages. He had been a great stepfather to my
daughter. How dare I complain that something was missing in
my life? How dare I advertise for Eros?

My parents were dying and I was growing unimagin-
ably older, but was that a reason to pursue what my old friend
Isadora Wing had called "the zipless fuck"? You betcha. It was
either that or spiritual bliss. Apparently the creators of Zipless
.com had ripped off Isadora without paying a penny. The company that bought her movie rights was sold to a company that
owned publishing rights, which was sold to a company that
exploited digital rights that was sold to a company that
exploited well-known tags. Such is the writing life—as savage
as the acting life.

Isadora and I had been friends forever. We met over a
movie that was never made. We even got sober together. And
I could call her for moral support whenever I needed her. I
thought of her as my BFF, my alter ego. I really needed her now.

———

I am going over to my parents' apartment to visit them, and I dread it. They have deteriorated drastically in the last few months. They both spend their days in bed attended by aides and caregivers. They both wear diapers—if we're lucky. Their apartment smells of urine, shit, and medications. The shit is the worst. It's not healthy shit like babies produce. It seems diseased. Its fetid aroma permeates everything—the oriental rugs, the paintings, the Japanese screens. It's impossible to escape—even in the living room.

When I get there, to my great relief, I realize my mother is having a good day. She's her old feisty self. Lying in bed, wearing a lilac satin negligee and wiggling her yellow-nailed toes, she blurts out:

"Who are you going to marry next?"

"I'm married to Asher," I say. "We've been married for fifteen years. You know that."

"Are you happy?" my mother asks, looking deep into my eyes.

I debate this unanswerable question. "Yes," I say. "I'm happy."

My mother looks at my rings—the gold art nouveau disk, the carnelian signet ring from Greece, the Victorian pierced aquamarine from Italy.

"If you got married again, you could get some more rings," she says, and laughs uproariously.

My mother is deep into her nineties and her cheerful dementia is studded with piercing insights. She is also much nicer than she was when I was young. Along with the crepey neck, the sagging arms, the bunioned feet has come a sweetness interspersed with a fierce truth telling. Sometimes she thinks

I am her sister or her mother. The dead and the living are all alive in her head. But she looks at me with an endless love I wish I could have taken for granted when I was young. My whole life would have been different. Or so I think. The truth is she often terrified me when I was young.

People shouldn't get this old. Sometimes I think my mother's senescence is taking years off my life. I have to force myself to look at her. Her cheeks are sallow and crosshatched with a million wrinkles. Her eyes are rheumy and clotted with buttery blobs. Her feet are gnarled and twisted, and her thick, ridged toenails are a jagged mustard color. Her nightgown keeps opening to reveal her flattened breasts.

I think of all the times I've sat in hospital rooms with my mother in the last few years. I am praying fiercely for her not to die. But aren't I really praying for *myself*? Aren't I really praying not to be the last one standing on the precipice? Aren't I really praying not to have to dig her grave and fall in?

As you get older, the losses around you are staggering. The people in the obits come closer and closer to your own age. Older friends and relatives die, leaving you stunned. Competitors die, leaving you triumphant. Lovers and teachers die, leaving you lost. It gets harder and harder to deny your own death. Do we hold on to our parents, or are we holding on to our status as children who are immune from death? I think we are clinging with ever-increasing desperation to our status as children. In the hospital you see other children—children of fifty, of sixty, of seventy—clinging to their parents of eighty, ninety, one hundred. Is all this clinging *love*? Or is it just the need to be reassured of your own immunity from the contagion of the Maloch ha-moves—the dread Angel of

Death? Because we all secretly believe in our own immortality. Since we cannot imagine the loss of individual consciousness, we cannot possibly imagine death. I thought I was searching for love—but it was reincarnation I really sought. I wanted to reverse time and become young again—knowing everything I know now.

"What are you thinking about?" my mother asks.

"Nothing," I say.

"You're thinking you never want to get as old as I am," she says. "I know you."

My father is sleeping through all this. His wasted body takes up remarkably little space under the blankets. With his hearing aid turned off, he cannot follow our conversation and he doesn't want to. He prefers to spend the day sleeping. Just six months ago, before his cancer surgery, he was a different man. My sisters and I used to start the day with threatening missives from him, often in verse.

What do you do when your days open with this messily penned screed from your ninety-three-year-old father?

I feel like King Lear.
I have three daughters
beautiful and dear,
clever and cute,
already in dispute.
Who gets more?
Who gets less?
What a terrible mess
For an aging Lear
In geriatric stress.

So much for poetry. At the bottom of the page he has scrawled in a shaky hand: "Read it again and again—no disputes!"

How did our father go from Brownsville to Shakespearean tragedy?

Here's his version: "All my father ever said to me was 'Get a job.' I wanted to go to Juilliard. My father said: 'You're already making money playing the drums—why do you need it?' He threw away my admission letter. That was why I was determined that the three of you should get degrees."

My father said this in my mother's studio overlooking the Hudson. She was lying in bed like Queen Lear, nodding. (*Was there a Queen Lear?*)

The sisters Lear were sitting around their mother's bed. Their mother had just had stomach surgery and she was making the most of it. Occasionally she moaned.

"Your mother has Crohn's disease, coronary artery disease, a fractured vertebra at the base of the spine, two hip replacements, two knee replacements. I cannot continue my job as 'U.S. male nurse' "—my father's pathetic phrase for his status in the family. "If you three don't come here every day, there will be some changes made in my will."

"Don't you dare threaten me," my older sister, Antonia, said. "When we were living in Belfast at the height of the Troubles"—of course Antonia had to marry a poetic Irishman—"pulling the piano in front of the door to keep the paramilitaries out, shopping for bread during the early-morning hours before the shooting started, covering the windows with furniture so that your grandchildren wouldn't get hit by shrapnel—where were you? We were going through a genuine holocaust and nobody came to rescue us. I'll never forgive any of you for that!"

Queen Lear suddenly revived: "What do you mean? We sent you money!"

"You sent us a measly twenty-five thousand dollars! What was I going to do with twenty-five thousand dollars with four children and a war going on?"

"Nobody ever sent *me* twenty-five thousand dollars," my younger sister, Emilia, said.

"No, your husband got the *whole* business. That's why you didn't need twenty-five thousand dollars!" Toni shrieked.

"Your husband didn't *want* the business! Nobody wanted it! We got stuck with it! You were both away gallivanting around the world and we were here, taking care of everybody! And Bibliomania—the shop itself. When Grandmama died, I was alone with her! The parents took off for Europe. Where were you two? I never got to go *anywhere*."

"That's not quite true," I said.

"Girls, girls, girls," my mother said.

"Nobody has any sympathy for me!" Emmy howled. "I felt I had to be the good daughter and stay home. I sacrificed my poor schnook of a husband on the altar of the family bookstore!"

"That poor schnook got everything! And so did you! We got nothing!" Toni wailed. "Some sacrifice!"

"I would have made that sacrifice."

"No way! You never would have done it. Your husband never would have done it!" This is Emmy, who shouted just as loud.

"Can't you try to see each other's point of view?" I asked.

"Not as long as she's a dishonest liar!" Toni yelled.

"My blood pressure's going up—I have to get out of here!" Emmy ran to the door. I dashed to her and coaxed her not to leave.

"Why shouldn't I leave? This is going to kill me! My heart's pounding!"

By then my father, the old King Lear, had gone to the piano and was playing "Begin the Beguine" by Cole Porter and singing along to drown out the roar in the other room.

I was where I always was—the meat in the sandwich, the designated peacemaker, the diplomat, the clown, the middle sister.

My sisters went into the kitchen to continue their altercation without a mediator. I went into my mother's room, where I found her leaning back on her pillows and moaning: "*Why* are they fighting?"

"You know perfectly well why," I said. "Daddy set it up that way."

"Your father would *never* do a thing like that," my mother said.

"Then make him undo it."

"I can't make him do anything," she said. And then she clutched her chest. "I feel faint," she said, rolling her head to the side. She moaned loudly.

My sisters ran in.

"Call the ambulance!" Emmy ordered me.

"I don't need an ambulance," my mother said, wailing.

My sisters looked at each other. Who would be the irresponsible one who neglected to call the ambulance on the ultimate day? Nobody wanted that onus.

"I really think it's unnecessary," I said, but my sisters' panic was beginning to stir the old anxiety in me. What if it was not a false alarm this time?

Before long there was an ambulance downstairs and we were in it, bending over Queen Lear on a stretcher in the back. Our father was in the front seat with the driver, prepared to flash his big-donor card when we arrived at the hospital. We careened around corners, screeching our way to Mount Sinai. On one abrupt turn the mattress from the gurney went slithering into the attendant sitting behind the driver.

"Oops," he said.

"Be careful! That's the only mother I've got!" I said.

"She's my mother too!" said Emmy—always pissed off no matter what the occasion.

Our father sat by our mother's side as long as she was hospitalized, and when she came home, he began threatening us with being disinherited unless we came to visit her every day.

Now, only months later, he is too exhausted to threaten us and I yearn for his old truculence. Ever since the surgery for the blockage in his colon, he has been a shade of his former self. I sit on the edge of the bed, watch him sleep, and remember the conversation we had in the hospital the night before the operation that saved yet also ended his life.

"Do you know Spanish?" my father asked me that night.

I nodded. "A little."

"*La vida es un sueño*," he said. "Life is a dream. I look forward to that deep sleep." And then he went under and never quite came back. Three days after the surgery he was babbling gibberish and clawing the air. Six days after the surgery he was in the ICU with a tube down his throat. When he was diagnosed with pneumonia, I stood at his side in the ICU and sang "I gave my love a cherry" while his eyelids fluttered.

We never thought that he would emerge from that hospitalization. But he did. And now he and my mother spend their
days sleeping side by side in their apartment but never touching or speaking. Round-the-clock shifts of aides and daughters
attend them. Every day they sleep more and wake less.

The ancient Greeks believed that dreams could cure you. If
you slept in the shrine of Aescalepius, you could dream yourself well. But my parents are not getting well. They are deep
into the process of dying. Watching them die, I realize how
unprepared for death I am myself.

It doesn't matter how old they are. You are never prepared
to lose your parents.

Even my sisters have tried vainly to make peace with each
other now that we have entered this final stage. We seldom go
to an event where some aged acquaintance doesn't get carried
out on a stretcher.

No wonder I was advertising for Eros. I was advertising
for life.

2

My Father (Boy Wanted)

There is a dignity in dying that doctors should not
dare to deny.

—Anonymous

There is no substitute for touch. To be alive is to crave it. The next day, when I go to visit my parents I decide I will not even try to talk to my father, I will only stroke him, rub his back, and try to communicate with him this way.

I ring the doorbell and am greeted by Veronica, the main day person. She's a Jamaican woman in her sixties with a lilting voice and a family history that could break your heart. Her son has died. Her daughter has MS. Yet she soldiers on, tending the dying.

"How's my father?"

"He's okay today," she says.

"Is he sleeping?"

"Not sleeping, not waking," she says. "But on his way somewhere . . ."

I go to his bedside and begin to massage the back of his neck.

"Who's there?" my mother says. "Antonia? Emilia?"

"It's me, Vanessa," I say. And I rub my father's neck until he stirs.

He mumbles: "I feel the love in your touch." This encourages me to go on until my arms are tired. As I massage him I am taken back to the time he sat on my bed when I was six and told me he would never leave my mother because of me. My parents had had a huge fight and I was terrified they'd divorce. My father quieted my fears.

"I would never leave you," he said.

My sisters have always accused me of being his favorite. But what good did that do me? A marital history of searching fruitlessly for him in the wrong partners until I married someone I thought could be his stand-in. And now we are all old and so is our story.

About a year ago, when my father was still robust enough to threaten us with being disinherited, I had come over to find him in an ebullient mood.

"Did I ever tell you about my first job?" he asked.

"No."

"Well, I walked around the neighborhood looking for signs in the windows that said 'Boy Wanted.' When I found one, I walked right in and said: 'I'm the boy you want.' I knew even then that your own enthusiasm had to carry the day. It was the same with show business. The reason I got the job in *Jubilee* when I auditioned for Cole Porter was because I had so much enthusiasm. I wasn't the best musician. I was only the most enthusiastic."

"Maybe he thought you were cute," my mother said. "He also had a sign out that said 'Boy Wanted.' Everyone knew that."

"You don't know what you're talking about," he said to my

mother. And then, in a burst of sheer bumptiousness, he began to do jumping jacks there on the bedroom floor. He did
about thirty in a row.

"Look at your father," my mother said. "He thinks if he
keeps exercising he'll never die." And it was true. My father
worked out as if his life depended on it. All through his eight-
ies, he walked to the bookstore every day, then came home
to walk another five miles on the treadmill. He was full of
contempt for our mother because of her sedentary life. He
starved himself down to a skeletal weight.

"Learn to go to bed hungry," he told me. "The thinner you
are, the longer you live. It's been proven." He ate sparingly but
gorged on vitamins. The dining room table was full of sea-
weed extract and HGH and all manner of trendy supple-
ments. But there came a day when he could barely eat at all
because of the pain.

My sisters and I went with him for the CAT scan, the sono-
grams, the X-rays. He sat in a little dressing room in the
radiologist's office shivering in his shorts and T-shirt. He
looked so small, so scared, so reduced. Nothing showed up on
the films. Finally they put him in the hospital and gave him
a colonoscopy, which found the blockage.

He was avid for the operation. "Cut it out. Get the bastard," he said. He believed that if they got the cancer, he'd
be good as new.

How many times have I seen that avidity for the knife?
"Cut it out," they say, as if mortality were no more than a tumor. But if death can't march in the front door, it'll sneak in
the back. They excised the cancer from his gut, but the anesthesia invaded his brain.

The first day after the surgery he was fuzzy but fine. As

in the old days on our family car trips, we sang our way through the alphabet from "All Through the Night" to "Zip-a-Dee-Doo-Dah." But the following morning he was holding *The New York Times* upside down in one hand and making up bizarre stories to explain the headlines. After that, two burly guards appeared in his room because he had bitten the nurse. I talked him down and stroked his hand and he went to sleep. But the day after he became even more agitated. First they thought it was the meds, Klonopin or Haldol or the anesthesia, but then a convocation of doctors decided it was "something physical" making him tremble, rant, shake, and grasp the air. They intubated him, catheterized him, and took him to a step-down, then to the ICU. There I prayed for him to come back, and in a way he did. Now I wonder about the wisdom of such prayers. Life, I now know, is the step-down unit of all step-down units. The only cure for the agitation of life is death. And the cure, as they say, is worse than the disease.

"Stop," he says now, "you're hurting me." Can he hear my thoughts? I think so.

"Veronica!" he calls. "I want to go to the toilet." And Veronica comes to take him. When he emerges, he seems exhausted and curls into the fetal position again.

"Is he sleeping all day?" I ask Veronica later. She takes this as a slur on her professionalism.

"I told you before and I'll tell you again. He doesn't want to wake because he's depressed and he doesn't want to sleep because he's afraid he'll die in his sleep. So whenever he feels himself drifting, he thinks he has to use the toilet. It only happens fifty times a day. He can't stay and he can't go. I told your sisters the same thing. Why do you all keep asking?"

"Because we love him," I say.

"I know you do," Veronica says. "So leave him alone."

"But we want to help him."

"How you gonna help him die?"

How indeed? If I could give him that final draft of pain-less poison, I would. Or would I? When my grandfather asked for sleeping pills at ninety-six, I didn't have the nerve to pro-vide them. I have regretted my cowardice to this day.

How do you help anyone die? I read with amazement the stories of people who reached a certain point of illness or of age and decided it was time to die. It seems the height of both courage and cruelty. Courage because anything so counter-intuitive takes courage. And cruelty because it leaves your children wondering if they did something wrong. There's no act you can initiate that doesn't involve other people. We are all interwoven. Even the most rational suicide may come as a blow to someone else.

"Vanessa!" my mother cries out. "Where are you?"

I go in to my mother. My father is curled up beside her, nearly motionless.

"He never talks to me anymore," she says, pointing a bony hand at my father. "All those years he was the closest person in the world to me and now he doesn't even talk to me. What can you do?"

Until his operation, my father was always complaining that my mother was senile, but now, despite moments of memory loss, she seems far saner than he. She lies by his side all day, enduring the most terrible rejection. Fortunately, she can only focus on it intermittently.

Abruptly, my father gets up. "Veronica!" he screams. Ve-ronica runs in and takes him to the toilet again.

My mother looks at me. "I don't think he really has to go,"

she says. "I just think he wants to be alone in the bathroom with that woman."

"She's the nurse's aide," I say.

"Don't believe that malarkey," says my mother. "She's only pretending to be a nurse's aide so she can undress him. I'm wise to all her tricks. I wasn't born yesterday. But I pretend I don't know. One of these days, I'm going to throw her out of the house."

It wouldn't be the first time. When my mother was a little stronger last year, she fired people constantly. "Get out of my house, you big fat thing!" Sometimes: "You big fat black thing," she would scream—my mother, who had never been a racist in her prime. I told myself she was more rational now, but she was only weaker. She was biding her time. One of these days, she'd get up screaming like her old self and throw all the strangers out.

"If I should go with the High Class Angels, who'll take care of her?" my father used to rant in the old days when he was strong. The "High Class Angels" fascinated me. Whom did he mean? The Angel of Death? Or was he wrestling with angels as he slept, like Jacob?

And hearing about these mysterious angels, my mother would shriek: *"Nobody has to take care of me! I'll bury you all."*

Sometimes I think she may know more than she lets on.

"I've seen a lot of people die," Veronica says later, "but your father is one tough old bird. He's going to fight like hell before he leaves this earth. Your mother too. She never stops watching me. You know that time she fell out of bed and had to go to the hospital? She was worried I was doing something with your father. Don't believe she's out of it. She's more together than she looks."

"How can you stand this work?"

"Who's gonna do it if I don't? You girls? You gonna clean up the shit when it runs down their legs?"

I go in to my mother again.

"When did you get here?" she asks as if we had not seen each other before, as if we had not just been talking.

I sit on her side of the bed. My father is there but not there, asleep, awake, and drifting in between.

"You know, when you get old, you see that everything is a joke. All the things you were so passionate about don't mean a thing. You only did them to keep busy. I used to think it was important that I could dance better than other people, but now I see I was only fooling myself. I only did it to keep busy."

"I don't think that's true."

"It is. Even if you're well known, what difference does that make? It doesn't keep you from getting old and dying. People see you come into a restaurant and they say, 'Isn't that so-and-so?' Well, what good does that do *you*? Or *them*, for that matter. It's all a joke."

"But you still want to live, don't you?"

"To tell you the truth, I'm bored. I'm bored with everything. Even the things I used to love—like flowers—bore me. Everything except my children. In the end, that's all that matters, leaving children behind on the earth to replace you when you go. Why do you look so sad? What's the matter?"

"You know what's the matter. I don't like you to say you're bored with life."

"Do you want me to lie to you?"

Actually, yes, I think. Please tell me that life is worth living. Please tell me that all the hassle of getting up, getting dressed, is worth the trouble. I don't want to believe that life is only a joke. I don't think parents ought to tell that to their children. Odd that I am still expecting them to be parents.

"You still look very young," my mother says.

"There's a reason for that," I say.

"Good genes," my mother says.

"Good genes and a face-lift."

"I don't believe you've had a face-lift," my mother says.

"Have it your way," I say.

Before I started to watch my parents fade away, the scariest thing I ever did was plastic surgery. A female ritual like child-birth. It stacks up there with all the other female rituals— genital mutilation, foot binding, whalebone corsets, Spanx. I know men do plastic surgery too now—voluntarily—but it's different for men. Women feel they have no choice. Age still equals abandonment for women. A man can look like he's a hundred, be impotent and night blind, and *still* find a younger woman who never got over her daddy. But a woman is lucky to be able to go to the movies or bingo with another old bag. I considered plastic surgery as mandatory as leg waxing.

First I sent the doctor a check so large I would not be able to back out. Then I spent five months in utter terror. (The last month was the worst.) Then I got on a plane and flew to Los Angeles.

Arrived in the midst of mudslides and heavy weather. (This was two winters before the century turned.) Took a room surrounded by fog in a skyscraper hotel. The floaty fiftieth floor. (Maybe an earthquake would intervene and I wouldn't have to go through with it.) The next morning, early, after disinfectant ablutions, sans breakfast, I limo'ed to the clinic. My darling friend Isadora Wing came with me to give moral support. She waited for me.

The doctor's office was decorated in ice-cream colors and all the nurses had perfect *Mona Lisa* faces done by him. They smiled their half-moon smiles. They reassured me.

I was taken into a rose-colored room with soft lights and told to undress. I was given elastic stockings, paper slippers, a grasshopper-green gown, green cap. I had already prepared by scrubbing myself, my hair, even my *shadow*, with doctor-proffered potions. I garbed myself in these ceremonial clothes and lay back on a reclining chair, a sort of airplane seat for traveling through time. The anesthesiologist and surgeon arrived, also in grasshopper green.

I remember looking into the anesthesiologist's soft brown eyes and thinking, I wonder if he's a drug addict. . . . We talked about the methods by which unconsciousness would be achieved. He seemed to know plenty about them. Almost imperceptibly, a needle was inserted into one of the veins that branched over my hand. The colorless liquid carried me away like a euthanized dog.

I had picked my doctor because I had seen his work—or rather because I saw that his work was invisible. Most New York plastic surgeons specialize in the windswept look—*Gone With the Wind* face-lifts, I call them. You see them on the frozen tundra of the Upper East Side. Bone-thin women whose cheeks adhere to their cheekbones as if they were extremely well-preserved mummies. My doctor, born a Brazilian with a noble German name (my husband joked that his father must

have been the dentist at Auschwitz before hurriedly leaving
for the Southern Hemisphere with bags of melted gold fill-
ings), was famed for his tiny, invisible stitches. He was an
artist, not a carpenter. He could look at the sagging skin around
your eyes and see how to excise just enough, not too much.
He could make tiny, imperceptible cheek-tucks that erased
the lines of worry and age. He could raise your forehead back
into your twenties. He smiled sweetly as anyone would smile
anticipating gargantuan fees. This was a hundred-thousand-
dollar three-procedure day for him. I drifted off to the Land
of Nod.

Time collapsed on itself and died. I didn't. (But if I *had*, I
would never have known, would I?) I woke up in a back room
of the clinic with a nurse asking me how I felt. Parched.
Trussed as a Christmas turkey. With a pounding headache.
All over my head.

"Do you want to use the bathroom?"

"May I?"

"I don't see why not." She took my arm.

I lurched toward the bathroom, used the toilet but avoided
the mirrors. I felt as if I had died and been embalmed. Now
I felt mummified—as if my whole brain had been scooped
out through my nose, as if the embalmers had also carved out
my soul. Shuffled back to bed. Or the cot that served as a bed.

"How do I look?"

"Not bad, considering," said the nurse. "Are you hungry?"

"I think so."

"A good sign."

The tepid instant oatmeal tasted better than any breakfast I had ever had.

I thought to myself: I'm eating. I must be alive.

The next days—ice packs, immobility, a sense of suspended animation—were grim. The anesthesia lingered like a nightmare. I couldn't stay in. I couldn't go out. I couldn't read. All I could do was watch the Olympics on TV. I am convinced that long hours of TV-watching actually lower your IQ. Television isn't about content. It's about flickering light keeping you company in an empty room.

I recovered to the tune of double axel and triple Lutz. The figure skaters might as well have been skating on my face, given the way I felt. There was nothing to do but stare at the TV and change my ice packs. I ordered consommé and ice cream from room service. I had dreams in which I saw my skin (complete with muscles and blood vessels) being pulled back from my skull. One night, I was awakened in the hotel by fire alarms and a recording announcing, "There appears to be a fire alarm activated. Please stand by for further instructions." This was repeated for two hours at intervals of seven minutes while I madly called the front desk, getting a busy signal. When I finally got through to him, the concierge pronounced a false alarm. But it was all worth it. After all the bruises were gone, I noticed an uptick in passes made at me.

If life is nothing but a joke, why did I bother with the face-lift?

"I can't believe you've had a face-lift," my mother insists. "You're too smart to have had a face-lift."

"Apparently not," I say.

"And has it given you a new lease on life?" my mother ironically asks.

"What do you think, Mrs. Wonderman?"

"Don't Mrs. Wonderman me," my mother says. It was an old family line. My father would use it ironically when he was most furious with my mother. Their marriage was tight but occasionally cantankerous, not unlike my marriage to Asher. How did I get here? How did I get to be Vanessa Wonderman? And what did Vanessa Wonderman want? Love, sex, immortality—all the things we can never have. What is the arc of the plot of one's life? I want! I want!

But what did I want? I wanted sex to prove that I would never die.

3

Wondermans Rampant

The only "ism" Hollywood believes in is plagiarism.

——Dorothy Parker

In their prime, the Wondermans led a glamorous life in the penthouse on Riverside Drive once owned by George Gershwin. They gave glittering parties where famous faces were glimpsed in smoke-filled rooms. "A tinkling piano in the next apartment / Those stumbling words that told you what my heart meant." I thought those lines were written for my parents; they certainly evoked my feelings about their parties—where ladies in satin and marabou smoked cigarettes in holders, clinked champagne glasses, drank in a way nobody drinks anymore, and changed husbands as they changed platform shoes. The men had darkly mirrored hair and thin mustaches like Adolphe Menjou. Limousines circled the block, awaiting them. Chauffeurs were black and wore caps. Maids were black and pretended to be obsequious. They put on their hats when they went home for the day.

When McCarthyism ended their show-biz careers and my parents returned from Hollywood at the height of the Blacklist, they found the Gershwin duplex and filled it with three decades' worth of memorabilia. It was a movie set as much as an apartment. Even the floor in the gallery was mirrored for exhibition dancing. The double grand pianos were lacquered white. The library had framed pictures of them from all their movies and leather-bound copies of all their scripts. The powder room off the gallery was an infinite hall of mirrors where I could stare at innumerable multiples of myself becoming greener and hazier with each reflection.

I never really knew how the Blacklist had affected them. They had plenty of friends who were also ruined by it, but my parents were too fiercely ambitious—even in the engagé thirties—to have signed the wrong petitions. The Blacklist coincided with the end of their salad days as performers. It was time to do something else anyway.

So they came back and set up Hollywood on the Hudson. They had smartly squirreled away their Hollywood money (despite what Dorothy Parker said about it melting in the palm like snow), and eventually their theatrical book and autograph shop, Bibliomania, also prospered. In a business—rare books—populated by nerds and ladies in Boston marriages, my parents were unusual. They had a flair for the dramatic and a flair for mixing people. Many couples fell in love at their parties. It was as if their love were contagious.

For three little girls in black velvet dresses and British black patent-leather Mary Janes that had to be fastened with button-hooks who watched from halfway down the stairs at their parties, it seemed that our parents were the King and Queen of Cool. It seemed we'd never live as glamorously as they. And it seemed the height of ambition to grow up and *become* our parents.

Now I know that many children feel that way. And that the lucky ones are the ones who outgrow it. Toni, Emmy, and I had never outgrown it. That was why our lives were so hard. We weren't starving or drinking polluted water, but we were stuck in a kind of emotional poverty all the same.

What struck me always, sitting at my parents' bedside, was that it was time for me to take off the black velvet dress and stop sitting in the middle of the stairs.

It was at one of my parents' parties that I first decided I was going to be an actress. All because of Leporello Kahn. I was sixteen when I met Lep Kahn (at the time the pun was lost on me). Lep—whose father was a famous opera singer at the old Met—was originally named after Don Giovanni's side-kick. It was a lousy thing to do to a child. Lep's name was a joke, so he tried to turn his life into a joke. He grew up to be one of those merry, seemingly harmless plump middle-aged men who brilliantly know how to appeal to teenage girls. He was the first man to let me know I was beautiful, and he was so suave and clever that he promptly made all the sixteen-year-old boys I knew seem like louts. (Not that it was hard.)

I met Lep at one of the first parties at which I actually drank vodka (in slavish imitation of my mother). I was wearing a strapless peony-pink gown with a harem skirt (those were the days of harem skirts), and with every drink, my breasts bobbled farther out of my boned top. Lep was looking at my breasts and saying, "You must come down to the Russian Tea Room and have lunch with me." The Russian Tea Room meant show business glamour in those days. Now it has morphed into an unrecognizable simulacrum—like everything else connected with that vanished world.

Lep was an important Broadway producer who did everything from Shakespeare to Pinter. A big *macher*. He promised me Juliet in a new production of *Romeo and Juliet*, and though the role fell through, my affair with Lep did not.

Without Lep Kahn, would I have had an abortion at sixteen, quit school at seventeen, moved to the Village, and appeared as Anne in the road show of *The Diary of Anne Frank* at eighteen (the part that deluded me into thinking that the theater was a viable profession)? No. No. No. No. Looking back, I should have stayed at Walden (which was loose enough to accommodate all kinds of hanky-panky), finished high school, gone to some arty college like Bennington or Bard, and never gotten involved with Lep Kahn—but who could have known that at the time? His passion for me seemed like the key to the life I wanted.

He was one of those attractive plump men. His stomach shook when he laughed in the nude. He had breasts almost as big as mine. But he also had melting brown eyes and long silky black lashes, wore wonderful tweed jackets, had a beard and mustache peppered with gray (which gave him an authoritative air), smoked a meerschaum pipe, and smelled of honeyed tobacco and Old Spice (sexy, then). He chewed cinnamon-and-clove gum—which I found harmlessly eccentric. I didn't think he was fat. He seemed Falstaffian to me—especially since he could quote Shakespeare by the yard. He was what I did instead of my senior thesis.

"'But, soft! What light from yonder window breaks? . . . It is the east, and Juliet is the sun. . . .'"

Imagine having that quoted to you while you are playing hooky from high school to drink vodka and eat blini with beluga at the Russian Tea Room—always thinking you will be

glimpsed with Lep by one of your parents' friends! The fear
of exposure was part of the thrill.

Since Lep was the reason I quit school at seventeen, having had an abortion at sixteen, you might say he was a child
molester who ruined my life. But I didn't think so at the time.
I was so excited about becoming an adult and an actress. I
assumed the couch casting came with the territory. Lep
arranged the abortion, in fact—back in the days when it was
illegal—with one of those show business doctors who practiced
right down the block from the Russian Tea Room.

However grown up I felt sneaking off to meet Lep at the
RTR and then going to his pad (as he called it) on Broadway
and Fiftieth Street in a big old gloomy apartment that also
served as his office, imagine how scared I was going off to get
an illegal abortion without my parents' knowledge. How alone
in the world I felt! Though Lep went with me and held my
hand. Even paid for it. I think he got me the Anne Frank role
because he felt so guilty.

Which of these tableaux should I present? The abortion
doctor's seedy office? Lep's gloomy, cavernous apartment
facing a courtyard filled with filthy pigeons nesting? Lep
dancing naked with his belly shaking?

Sex with him was not amazing, but I had nothing to compare it to at the time. He knew how to eat pussy, though—
perhaps to make up for the fact that his penis was not always
operational in those pre-Viagra days. He compensated for the
softness of his prick with the hard truth of poetry. And then
with the part of Anne Frank, who in those days represented all
innocence, beauty, truth—the summit of every young actress's
desire.

I see myself at sixteen, walking hand in hand with Lep into

the abortion doctor's lair, sure I would be dead by nightfall. (Everybody then had heard of a girl who died from—or was sterilized by—a botched abortion.)

No nurse was present. No receptionist. Abortions were done then without the benefit of witnesses or anesthesia. I dressed in a gown (as later for my face-lift), lay on the table with bare feet in the cold stirrups, gratefully accepted the shot of whiskey proffered, and fell into a red hole of pain so excruciating I can feel it to this day. I can still remember my womb horribly cramping, still remember retching and nearly choking on my vomit, still remember the doctor shushing me. When I asked for Lep, the doctor told me that he had "gone to a meeting"—which in those days had nothing to do with AA—but had sent a car for me.

I see myself then, pale, shaking, drained of hope, in the back of a Cadillac limousine, trying to be brave, trying not to cry for my mother, trying to feel as grown up as I had had lunching with Lep at the RTR. But it was no use. I was a mess. Relieved, yes. But my head was unaccountably full of visions of pink babies, my heart a hollow nest, my rage buried in a million excuses for Lep (he had a meeting, had a deal to do, responsibilities to escape because they were too painful). I had more mercy on him than I had on myself.

Those were the good old days of either-or. Either be an actress or have children. Either succumb to fluffy, eventually soul-destroying domesticity, or be a sleek woman with kohl-rimmed eyes who was far too sophisticated to *confess* to wanting a baby. Either Kate Hepburn or the happy housewife—there was no in-between. Every choice available to women meant pain and renunciation. My daughter's generation, who turned their backs on their brilliant careers to make brilliant babies, learned that by and by. A woman without a paycheck becomes a slave in a world that worships Mammon. Woo-hoo! Could have told 'em that. But would they listen? Do daughters ever listen to mothers or mother-figures? No. You can't tell no one nothing! Remember that and shut up. Half of parenting is keep your piehole, as the Brits call it, *sealed*. It's a Monty Python world—and the Sermon on the Mount is rewritten by Lloyd Blankfein and Jamie Diamond. Don't turn the other cheek unless you want your pocket picked. And so it goes.

But maybe *I* am rewriting history. Now that I am sixty and my eggs and my acting career are all washed up, every child I did not have cries out to me like a ghost on a cloud seeded with shadowy infants. But what did I know then? Did I know my parents would get old and ill? I wouldn't have believed it possible. They seemed so powerful then.

Not long ago I read in the *Times* that Lep Kahn had died. Good, I thought, now nobody will know. My secret is safe with him. The abortion doctor died long ago.

So we grew up in the Never-Neverland of forties Hollywood and we returned to New York in the fabulous fifties. We all remembered trick-or-treating by limousine with movie stars' kids. We remembered Halloween costumes borrowed from the studios. We could still smell the eucalyptus trees of Westwood and hear the crashing Pacific of Malibu and Trancas. We were California kids transplanted to New York and the transplant never quite took. Sometimes I think that is why all three of us long for Mediterranean landscapes. Toni found hers and Emmy fell hopelessly in love with Italy. And I was bicoastal before the word was coined. I batted back and forth between New York and L.A. like a Ping-Pong ball for most of my professional life. The place I felt most at home was the air in between. I belonged nowhere. Often I still feel that way.

When I married Asher, my acting career had gone to that place women's acting careers used to go when they neared fifty. There were no interesting jobs for me, so I quit. I refused to play the mother, then the grandmother, then the crazy old hag. I became Asher's wife with a vengeance. And since Asher was seemingly rich, my job as wife was all-consuming. We entertained in Litchfield County, at the beach, in Manhattan, in the Luberon. I was the perfect hostess and event-planner—a profession in itself. Probably the oldest profession—but for that other one. The days slipped by. Once you get off the career train, it's not so easy to get back on. I let my contacts slip.

Of course, if I were still working, I wouldn't have to advertise for sex. When you are actively employed in the profession, men turn up routinely. They may be less than men—actors—but they know how to *play* men. That's their craft. They are especially good at brief and dangerous liaisons. Permanence scares them. Which all worked very well for me as long as *I* was scared of permanence.

Thinking back to all the brief and dangerous liaisons I had on the job, I doubt that I'd be able to have them now—even if I were working. It takes a certain optimism to begin an affair—an optimism I may have lost. You have to believe that another man will make it better. And that gets harder and harder as you get older.

I hate getting older. I don't see anything good about it. The downward slope of life is full of rocks. Your skis are blunt and there are these patches of black ice everywhere, ready to slip you up. They may have been there before but you never noticed them. Now they are lying in wait for you on every slope.

Vanessa Wonderman had a great career from Anne Frank on. I played Juliet, Viola, Miss Julie, Maggie the Cat, and dozens of murdered girls in movies. Those were the days when women were mostly victims. (Actually, that hasn't changed as much as we had hoped.) But dying was a living. Until I got too old to be an attractive corpse.

No doubt about it, I was going through a bad patch. I wanted to shake myself. This was no way to live—or to die.

And then an e-mail came from the Zipless ad that piqued my interest:

> I love that you describe yourself as a happily married
> woman. I've always thought that a happily married
> woman would make the best lover. I cannot celebrate
> Eros once a week because I live far from New York,
> but perhaps I could manage once a month. Will you meet
> me for a drink at my favorite restaurant in New York and
> check me out? No strings, just a drink. Fear not,
> I am happily married too.

I carried the printed e-mail around in my purse for several weeks. Just having it in my possession made me feel vaguely hopeful—as if my erotic life was not over, as if there was still hope for me. Then, impulsively, I wrote to the e-mail address given:

    HMW desires your photo.

    Almost instantly I received a jpeg of a rather handsome brown-haired man with a salt-and-pepper beard and big blue eyes. He looked to be about forty. "Call me," his e-mail said. A number was proffered.

    So I did. He sounded nice. We had a pleasant if somewhat awkward conversation.

    "Will you meet me next time I'm in New York?" he asked.

    "Why not?" I said.

    "Why not *yes* or why not *no*?"

    "Yes."

    It was either that or the black ice.

    Asher would hardly be happy if I succumbed to suicide. Sex was better than suicide, and this wasn't even sex—it was just a drink.

    We meet at '21', under the ceiling of boys' toys. I have no idea what to expect. Naturally, I am nervous. I debate whether to use my real name and decide against it. I hold a white rose as the agreed-upon sign that I am me.

    A tall, handsome man with startling blue eyes walks in, also holding a white rose. He looks around the bar room until he finds me, seated in a corner. He pulls up a chair.

    "You must be HMW," he says.

    "I am."

    "I am HMM—Happily Married Man."

    "So I see."

    "I'm very glad you came," he says. Then there is a pause. We can't figure out what else to say.

"Will you tell me your real name?"

"Yes: David. And yours?"

"I'm not ready to tell you that."

"So what should I call you?"

"Call me Serena. Perhaps it will have a magical effect."

"I hope so. Tell me why you placed that ad. I'm really curious."

"Well, I adore my husband, but he's much older, and people seem to be dying all around me."

"Sex is very lacking and you miss it, right?"

I feel guilty even nodding, so I say and do nothing in response.

"Tell me about you," I propose.

"My wife is ill. I'd feel like a cad if I left her, but my life is pretty bleak. I was hoping to banish the bleakness. I don't want to get involved with anyone who might know her or me, but I thought since I come to New York every so often. . . . So I saw the ad and thought I'd take the risk. I'm terrified actually."

"Me too." Was it possible we were perfect for each other?

"Can I buy you a drink?"

"Please."

He calls the waiter and we order drinks—red wine for me, bourbon for him.

"You're beautiful," he says, "and I'm sure I've seen you before."

"Unlikely."

"Why is it unlikely?"

"I've spent my whole life being an Upper East Side housewife," I lie. I have no intention of identifying myself.

"Why is that bad?"

"In New York it's a crime never to have done anything with your life."

"I'm sure you've done things with your life. You wouldn't look so alive if you hadn't."

"Thank you. Do I really look alive? Some days I feel half dead."

"Everyone should look so good dead."

"What brings you to New York?"

"I'm raising money for my company, meeting with investment-fund managers, that sort of thing."

"Men in suits?"

"Yes, and a few women in suits, but I don't want to talk about that. I can do those pitches in my sleep."

"What do you want to talk about?"

"What we came here for—fantasy."

"Do you want to tell me yours?"

"I'd rather show you."

"I'd rather get to know you first."

"Often that ruins the fantasy."

"I'll take that risk."

"Look, why don't you come to my suite at the Palace—right down the block—and we'll talk there. I have a car waiting."

I think about it. It puts me in a sweat. He is a total stranger, and the idea of sex with a total stranger terrifies me.

"But you're a total stranger."

"Then get to know me."

I battle with myself. At twenty, I would have been challenged, but now going to a hotel room with a strange man seems like the sheerest folly. Am I going to risk all the great things I have with Asher for a perfect stranger?

"My father is dying," I say.

"All the more reason why you should live."

"Look—you go to your suite and order lunch and maybe I'll join you there if I find the courage." Am I ready for risk-taking or not? I used to be good at putting all the risks out of my head, but now I think about how much I have to lose.

"Good. Suite 2733."

He leaves. I run to the ladies' room, pee, touch up my makeup, and run down the block to Madison Avenue before I can change my mind. Then I circle the block three times in a daze, debating with myself. Am I ready for adventure or not? The old dybbuk of impulsiveness comes back. I will go to his suite. What do I have to lose except everything?

When I get there, a waiter is laying out a spread of beluga caviar, smoked salmon, and Champagne. The suite is huge and sunny. David is grateful I have come. When the waiter leaves, he kisses me decorously on the cheek. His beard is scratchy.

"No strings," he says, moving swiftly away.

We sit opposite each other at the table and toast in vintage Krug. He prepares me a toast point with caviar.

What am I doing here? I think in a panic. Nevertheless, we continue to make small talk as if we have just met at a cocktail party.

"All my life, I've dreamed of meeting a woman who shares my fantasies."

"We all dream of that."

"But some fantasies are more unusual than others."

"I'm sure we're all pretty much the same in the fantasy department."

"Not necessarily," he says. Then he stares at me and continues, "Dare I?"

"Dare you what?"

"Dare I share with you?"

"I don't see why not."

"Perhaps we should just have lunch and wait for my next visit."

"Fine with me. I can't stay very long today anyway."

"Oh—what the hell," he says.

He gets up and goes into the bedroom of the suite. A few seconds pass. When he returns he is holding aloft a black rubber suit with zippers over the crotch and the breasts. He looks at once sheepish and mischievous. He raises his eyebrows in question as if he is channeling Jack Nicholson. His beard makes him look Mephistophelian when he works his eyebrows that way. "What do you think?"

"Do *you* wear it? Or do *I*?"

"You. And there are certain accessories that go with it."

"Accessories?" My mind is blank. I don't think immediately of manacles and chains and whips, although the Marquis de Sade must have had such stuff at Lacoste—his ruined castle in the Luberon.

"You know," he says. "Accessories."

Then it dawns on me. He's thinking of gothic paraphernalia. My mind flies back to a time I played Sade's Justine, the twelve-year-old serving maid whose *virtu* is tested by nuns, monks, cavaliers, *comtes*—et cetera. Someone had adapted Sade's *Justine* into a filthy French movie.

Sade was a revolutionary, of course, with a revolutionary's detestation of the establishment. Did the monks preach virtue? Then he would preach sin. He was, we know, a member of the National Convention and hated hypocrisy as much as he hated its chief purveyor, the Catholic Church. For which he spent five years in the Bastille and thirteen years in Charenton, the insane asylum. Most of his books were written in jail—a terrific place for a libertine to write. Freedom, after all, is distracting.

In the only known portrait of him—done when he was twenty—he has such a sweet face. Jail may have saved his life in that bloody period when aristocrats were being guillotined. It certainly increased his literary output.

Oh, I had done S&M with the director of that movie—a certain Christian Fleuvier d'Anjou, who claimed to be a *comte* himself, descended from a distant cousin of Sade. It was a big bore to me—and dangerous to boot. Maybe the girls who'd never heard of "the Divine Marquis" or even *L'Histoire d'O* were turned on by it—especially if they got cash and prizes along with the stinging butt and reddened clit. But I much preferred soft lights and sweet music—tenderness, even if fake tenderness.

We all have our particular preferences. Mine is gentle sex, the kind in which a man takes forever before he touches you down there. But most people are so guilty about sex that they want the crime and the punishment built in.

"I think it's not my cup of tea," I say softly.

"Oh, just try it on," David pleads. "You never know till you try."

I don't know whether to laugh or cry. Nothing human is alien to me, but I don't want to wear that suit. God only knows what the matching headgear is. And I had already tried

S&M—as a young actress—with a director who turned out to be a horse's ass. And violent besides.

"I think I know," I say, getting up to go. "Thank you so much for the drink."

"You bitch," he hisses. "How could you lead me on like this?"

"I thought this was just *lunch*."

"I thought you were *serious*."

"I thought so too, but I never made any promises."

He grabs my arm and squeezes it painfully. "I can get younger chicks than you."

"I'm sure you can—let me go!"

"You're fifty if you're a day."

"Thanks, I'll tell my plastic surgeon. I'm sure he'll be pleased."

And somehow I make it to the door without his touching me again. I run to the elevator in a sweat. He doesn't follow. I descend to the lobby. I walk several blocks at a trot, always thinking there is a stretch limousine following me. My high heels clatter over the pavement. I am already out of breath.

How could you be so stupid? You know the world is full of crazy people who have learned how to temporarily hide their craziness. Scratch a lover and find a lunatic! And then I flag down a cab and go to see my parents.

"I'm a hundred and ninety-three and half dead!" my father raves. "Same old story."

Veronica has made him get up and sit at the table for tea and he is pissed off.

"What is the matter with your father?" my mother asks me.

"You married him, I didn't," I say.

"But he is so grouchy," she says. "He's never been this grouchy."

I go and kiss my father on his head. "Same old story," he says dismissively. "I know what you're here for."

"What?"

"Money."

"I am not. I don't want your money."

"Bullshit," my father says, and begins fiddling to turn off his hearing aid.

"Don't you *dare* turn off that hearing aid, Mr. Wonderman," Veronica says. "Vanessa is here to see you."

"What for? I'm half dead. I ought to jump out the window." He gets up and walks toward the dining room window, but Veronica restrains him.

"You ought to count your blessings," she says. "Look down the street at the homeless people. You got it good. You got to get you some gratitude."

"Gratitude, platitude," my father growls.

"At least he can still rhyme," says my mother.

"Let me go back to bed!" my father screams. "I've been awake long enough!" He is Dylan Thomas raging against the dying of the light, Ivan Ilyich in his black sack.

"He sleeps all the time," my mother says. "I don't understand it."

In movies the dying have long, intense conversations before parting, but it's not like that in real life—or is it? My father escaped from my mother the only way he could. He was escaping from her in sleep as he had once escaped from her in work.

"I do," I say. I have only been there five minutes and already I'm longing to leave.

I think of the rubber suit and suddenly begin to laugh.

"What are you laughing at?" my mother asks as my father is frog-marched down the hall to his bedroom, a prisoner in striped pajamas.

"Nothing."

"Some nothing. *Tell* me."

"I'm thinking that if we have to see the world as a tragedy or a comedy, we might as well see it as a comedy. It's more fun."

"I agree with you," my mother says. I long to tell her about the rubber suit. She would see the absurdity of it. Even in her present condition.

My phone vibrates then. I sneak a peek. It's from my swain with the rubber suit—or at least I think it is.

"You bitch!" he's texted; the creep now has my cell phone number.

"Are you happy, darling?" my mother suddenly asks. She has become as angelic as my father was demonic.

"Don't I look happy?" I ask.

"You look worried," my mother says. "A mother can always tell."

I go into the other room and call my friend Isadora. "I'm visiting my parents and I need a drink," I say over the phone.

"That's the last thing you need. What's happening?"

"My parents are dying and I met a man who wants me to wear a rubber suit for him."

Isadora breaks into gales of laughter. "I must have met him too once upon a time—or his twin brother. He'll do you as little good as a drink."

"Come—meet me for coffee. We can compare notes."

When Isadora bounces into the espresso place where we always meet, I'm struck again by her curly blond hair and big smile, as if she is thirty, not sixty. Seeing her makes me feel that getting older is not so terrible.

Isadora and I like to meet in a tiny coffee shop where the espresso is supposed to be the best in the city. It's a hole in the wall on the Upper East Side but the coffee is indeed extraordinary. We both order lattes.

"Rubber suit?" asks Isadora.

"Rubber suit," I say.

"How do you know you wouldn't like it?"

"I know," I say. "Have you ever worn one?"

"I refuse to answer on the grounds it might tend to incriminate me. I know that most people who have read my books think I've tried everything. I let them think so."

"But it's not true?"

"What do you think?"

"I think you're just a nice Jewish girl pretending to be a sex fiend," I say.

Isadora laughs. "At one point in my life I may have been a love junkie, but it taught me a lot—and I would never be fooled by a site like Zipless now—even though I named it. Sex on the Internet is much overrated."

"Why?"

"Because most of the people drawn there are confusing fantasy with reality. They think they know what they want, but they don't."

"What do they really want?"

"Connection. Slow sex in a fast world. You can't get that from a woman in a rubber suit. Or a man."

I think about it. Isadora is right. We all want connection, and the velocity of our culture makes it harder and harder to find.

"What you really want," my dear friend says, "is joy. Tell me when you find that—because you're looking for it in all the wrong places!"

4

Heartbeat

If I got rid of my demons, I'd lose my angels.

——Tennessee Williams

There are some women you meet and you know immediately you can trust them with your life. Isadora was my soul mate, protector, godmother to my tall, beautiful, redheaded daughter.

"You'll never regret having a daughter," she said—and she was right. I even blessed my crazy ex-husband for my daughter. She was the silver lining in the storm of my life, my daughter whom I love more than any human being on Earth, my daughter who can make me angrier than any human being on Earth, my darling actress daughter who can make me laugh until I cry, my daughter who is both thorn and balm for my heart. Now she is five months pregnant. When she calls, I jump.

"Mom, meet me at the doctor?"

"What time?"

"Twelve noon, sharp."

I get there at eleven-thirty (to avoid a daughterly tongue-lashing) and wait for my super-prompt daughter, who swans in at ten of twelve. "Why did you get here so early?" she demands.

"So I wouldn't be late and piss you off."

"You never piss me off," she laughs.

"Glinda?" the nurse announces.

"Can my mom come in with me?" Glinda asks.

"Of course."

Is this the place to tell you about Glinda's father? He was a poet and a playwright whom I adored when Glinda was born—before his jealousy of my love for the baby led him to abandon us both. I know he didn't want to abandon us and I often find myself hoping that this shared grandchild will somehow bring us to be friends again. He is an important witness to my life and Glinda's. Because of Glinda, I'll never regret him. His name was Ralph, but he had changed it to Rumi, somehow hoping to suggest he was a Persian poet and a dervish. Smitten with Sufism, he believed that all the world needed was peace. He frequently quoted Rumi's verses—particularly the one that goes something like this:

We may think we know ourselves.
We may be born Muslims, Jews, or Christians.
But until our hearts are healed
we see only differences.

He was such an idealist. He believed he could make the world a better place through poetry. In many ways, Glinda is like him.

Glinda and I go into the exam room, where the nurse fits

my daughter's belly with a fetal monitor and suddenly the whole room resounds with the rapid heartbeat of my grandson. This little creature who is destined to outlive us both fills the room with his thundering will to live.

"Does it sound normal?" Glinda asks Dr. Wilder, a pretty blond ob-gyn in her forties.

"Perfectly normal. Here, let me feel how you are." She reaches inside my daughter. "No problem."

"Damn," says Glinda, who has had a perfectly horrible pregnancy. Morning sickness day and night for five months, rashes, swollen hands and feet, not to mention genetic terrors in the first trimester. Both Glinda and her husband are Ashkenazic and had to wait until all the genetic tests were run. Glinda has been a heroine through all of this, but now she wants it over. She is praying for some condition that will make her doctors induce an early delivery. No such luck. The baby is already five pounds or more but not ready to hatch. In my family, we all have huge babies.

"Don't tell me what a great pregnancy you had with me!" Glinda says. Then to her doctor: "My mother always says she adored pregnancy. It infuriates me."

"All pregnancies are different, darling."

"Your mother is right," says the doctor.

Glinda glares at me as if she can't believe I'd ever be right about anything. "How can she be right when she named me after a witch?"

"It was either that or Ozma," I said. "I wanted you to live happily in the land of Oz."

"A good witch," says the doctor. "The Good Witch of the West."

Glinda rolls her green eyes.

"Dr. Wilder, I want an epidural the minute I go into labor."

"We don't torture women anymore," the doctor says.

"Good." I cannot bear the thought of Glinda being in pain. But I know how unpredictable labor is. I expect Glinda's baby to pop right out even though I myself had a C-section after nine hours of labor. I don't say this. There's nothing I can say and I know it. Half of motherhood is shutting up—as I said before. All I can say is I wish I'd known this earlier. Sometimes I think we should give every new mother an embroidered pillow that says what Kafka supposedly had over his desk: *Warten* (wait).

After the exam, Glinda and I go to lunch.

"I'm never having another baby," Glinda says. "I told Sam and he agrees."

"You don't have to ever have another one. One baby is fine. Nothing wrong with only children. Look at you." I know Glinda will change her mind a dozen times about this and everything else.

"I don't know how the human race ever survived," she says.

"It's astonishing, isn't it?"

I remember saying the same thing right after she was born. I was sitting in my hospital room watching a right-wing politician and a Catholic priest going on about the evils of abortion, and I threw the apple from my lunch tray right at the TV screen. Nothing broke. Nothing changed either.

I looked at the beautiful little creature in the plexiglass cradle and marveled at her perfection. Jaundiced, yes. Wrapped in a flannel blanket of pink and blue, wearing a unisex knitted cap like a yarmulke on her reddish curls—but perfect from toes to top of soft skull. She was both beautiful and terrifying. I wanted nothing but the land over the rainbow for her. I wanted her to inhabit the land that *I dreamed of once in a lullaby.*

"If men could get pregnant, abortion would be a sacrament," the feminists of my generation used to say. What had happened to all those feisty women? Where are they now when we need them most? Dead? How did the word "feminist" get to be an insult? All we wanted was to make an unfair world more fair.

Glinda didn't have to be convinced of any of this. She seemed to have inhaled feminism with my milk. At sixteen she quit school to star in a Brat Pack movie. At seventeen she won a Tony as a singing Juliet on Broadway. At eighteen she soared above the West End as Peter Pan. At nineteen she played the young Elizabeth the First of England in a wonderful film. But shortly thereafter she was at Hazelden detoxing from an addiction to coke.

She took to Hazelden as if it were her spiritual home. From the moment she found clarity, she never wanted to lose it again. She became a mentor to other kids in the program. Sobriety became more important to her than anything. I admired her tenacity and grit even more than I admired her acting—which was splendid.

"Mom, you should be working," she said over a chicken Caesar salad at Sarabeth's.

"You should be too."

"I will, as soon as the baby's launched. But you can't stop acting. It was your lifeline."

"I don't want to play grannies. I want to *be* a granny, not play one. Do you have any idea of the stupidity of the roles that are out there for women? The tragedy is that you get better and better at what you do—and the roles get worse. You feel confident of your craft for the first time—just before they throw you on the trash heap."

"Then produce your *own* stuff. Play King Lear as a woman. Get Asher to bankroll you. He would love it. He'll do anything to top his father." Asher's father had lost everything, which was one reason Asher had been so driven to accumulate money and power.

"Queen Lear? But my mother is Queen Lear. I'll have to wait for her to die!"

"No, I mean King Lear as a woman. Grab the good roles and play them. If casting is colorblind, why can't it be gender blind? It's a brave new world. Don't accept the crap they give you to play. Make up your own. Plunder Shakespeare or Marlowe or Shaw or write your own stuff. Work with your friend Isadora! Doctor Faustus as a woman conjuring up Adonis instead of Helen of Troy. You don't have to give up. I *hate* you giving up. Asher hates it too. He told me the other day that he thinks you're depressed and he wants you to work again. He really loves you."

"Finding roles at sixty?" I ask.

"Sixty is the new forty."

"And eighty is the new sixty. What does that make you at twenty-five? Five?"

"Probably. Mentally at least. My brain seems to have gone on hiatus since I got pregnant. Look, I need you *not* to give up. How am I going be sixty if you don't show the way?"

"You're right."

"Don't say I'm right and then go away and forget what I said. You're falling into a pit with Grandma and Grandpa."

"They're in their nineties and wear diapers—but I guess the nineties is the new seventies."

My cell phone pings with a text. I delete it without even looking.

"What's that?" Glinda asks. I don't answer.

"Every time I go to see them, I want to kill myself," I say.

"They've had long, full lives, daughters who love them, success beyond anyone's wildest dreams, no major illnesses. You have nothing to feel guilty about."

"Then why do I feel so guilty?"

"Because you're crazy. The fact is, you don't have to feel guilty about anything—not even me. You saved my life, Mommo. I will never forget that as long as I live. Now you really have to get back to work."

"Come on—you saved your own life. I couldn't have saved you if you were hell-bent on self-destruction."

"It was you, Mommo—you, you, you. But I really want you to get back to work. You *need* your work."

Glinda's acknowledgment takes me back nine years to another autumn—an autumn of maternal terror.

I remember four sudden insistent rings at the doorbell. (Only Glinda rings four times, so I know something is wrong. Glinda has followed in my footsteps and is supposed to be in L.A. shooting a movie.) The housekeeper answers. My beautiful nineteen-year old daughter bursts into the apartment sobbing.

"Mom," she says, "I think I'm going to die. You've got to listen!"

She is skeletally thin, her hands shake, and her hair hangs greasily over her wasted face.

My first thought is to say, "It can't be that bad," but something stops me. I don't want to believe my daughter is an addict—what mother does? But I realize both our lives may depend on my believing her. So I do the mother thing: shut up.

"Mommo—I don't sleep anymore—too wired. Then I take pills to come down. I'm afraid I'll be one of those people who never wake up. I'm turning into a coke whore. You have no idea how easy it is to be a coke whore in Los Angeles."

I never liked coke, so all this is hard to imagine, but I have enough friends with dead kids to believe her. I have friends whose kids jumped off buildings, inhaled CO_2, smashed up cars, sliced their wrists.

"I think I need to go to rehab. I really do. It terrifies me. I'll lose my movie. But otherwise I think I'll lose my life."

I hold her in my arms, smelling the sour smell of vomit. I remember her baby smell, her sweet head smelling of baby oil, her sweet pink tush smelling of baby crap. How can your children get so far away from where they started? Where do they go in adolescence? It's certainly not the Land of Oz. I immediately start making phone calls. By that night, Glinda and I are on a plane for Minnesota.

Even though it's November, Minnesota is frozen. Minnesota is always frozen. We are in baggage claim when a tall chubby man in a parka comes up to us.

"Glinda?" he hisses toothlessly. His skin is red, his head shaved and tattooed. Most of his teeth are missing.

"I'm Vanessa, this is Glinda."

"I'm your ride," he says. "I'm Cal W."

We get into a station wagon and drive north. It starts snowing hard. I hold Glinda's hand.

"I'm scared, Mommo."

"No reason to be scared," says toothless Cal calmly. "You're in the right place. You're where you belong."

I wonder if we'll ever get out of the frozen northern wastes. We drive and drive. Cal barely speaks—except to ask us if we need a bar or a bathroom.

"A bar?" I ask.

"Some folks like to tank up for the last time," he says.

"Please, no," says Glinda. "I never want to tank up again."

"I could use a bathroom," I say.

We park in front of a diner with a flashing neon sign that reads: MOM AND POP'S DINER—ALL U CAN EAT.

I go in to use the loo and wonder if Cal and Glinda will be there when I emerge. The bathroom smells of fake roses and shit. It has cutesy cartoons of dogs and cats on the walls.

On arrival, we seem to have entered the frozen tundra of America. The entrance to the building is down a snowy path. The place seems deserted, yet a few minutes after we press the bell, a handsome white-haired male nurse greets us. Glinda grabs my hand.

"I need to talk to Glinda alone now," he says. "You should probably wait outside."

"Don't go, Mommo."

"I think I should."

"Glinda," says the white-haired man, a counselor called Jim R., "I need to ask you some specific history of what brought you here, and I think you might be more comfortable talking if your mother isn't here."

"Okay" she says.

I wait outside in a cubicle, muttering prayers under my breath. I am full of remorse. How could I have let this kid go to L.A. alone? How could I have been so immersed in my own problems? Glinda stays with Jim R. an hour or so while my mind races. Then she comes out, her eyes red, her nose running. Jim and I walk her down the hall to Detox and there are papers to sign. Glinda is taken into a little room with a bed and a sink. Another nurse comes in and searches her luggage.

"Why don't you get some sleep?" she says. "We'll take good care of her."

"Go, Mommo, I'll be okay. I promise."

Much of the building we're in seems to be an underground earth burrow. Perhaps we'll turn into hobbits here? I love hobbits. I am escorted down a long underground corridor until we come to a warren of doors—all locked. Where is my earth burrow? Where are the friendly hobbits? My room is spartan—a single bed is bolted to the floor, as are the lamps. The bathroom has a paper bath mat and two tiny white towels, hobbit-size. I shed my clothes and crawl into the narrow bed. I am shaking.

"God help me," I mutter. "God, please be there, please."

There have been lots of times in my life when I felt I had hit bottom, but this is the lowest. Glinda is my future, all the dreams I have not fulfilled. I need Glinda to live more than I need to live myself.

When I wake up at five in the morning, I find my room looks out on a frozen lake. Little huts are set up on the ice. Small bundled figures are walking across, leaving tracks in the snow. It is the quietest place I have ever been. You can listen to your thoughts here. I quickly dress—my clothes are all wrong, of course—and walk outside in the snow. My thin shoes crunch and I can feel the cold straight through. Still, I find a path between the tall firs and I follow it as long as I can stand the cold. Then I reverse direction and come back. In one of the lounges of the building where my room is, I find a fire going in a stone fireplace and coffee and doughnuts laid out. I get some coffee and sit in front of the fire drinking it. I pick up a book called *Serenity* from one of the tables. Here are the words I open to: "When we stop thinking of fears and doubts, they begin to lose their power. When we stop believing good things are impossible, anything becomes possible."

"Did you find something interesting?" a fiftyish man asks me.

I look up. He has straw-blond hair, an unshaven jaw, and a stump where his right hand should be. I stare at it too hard.

"I'm sorry to stare," I say.

"How did I do it? Well, I was high on coke and hallucinating that God was telling me to cut my hand off. I did it with a Chinese meat cleaver—messily—my son found me losing blood, flesh dangling by a thread. I now think it was the best thing that ever happened to me. By the way, my name is Doug." He extends his left hand. We shake.

"Because it saved my life. It woke me up. Some people can only do it that way. What brought you here?"

"My daughter."

"Well, she's come to the right place. And you?"

"This is the most peaceful place I've ever been."

"It makes it clear how much of the noise is in your own head, doesn't it?"

"What do you do all day here?"

Doug laughs. "Believe me, you don't get bored. Chores, meetings, meals, talking to people, writing about your life for your counselor. The days fly. I've been here two months already. I never want to go home. I suspect I will, though."

"Are you afraid of a relapse?"

"That's why God gave me such a visible reminder." He shakes his stump. "Some of us can't do with subtle reminders."

"Do you really believe in God?"

"What's my choice? If there were no God, I would have died. Nobody would have found me until it was too late. There has to be some reason I'm walking around with this stump, don't you think? It sure gets everyone's attention. Look— everyone here has trouble with the God stuff. They come here after having demonstrated to themselves that they can't manage their own lives and then they go around bitching about whether or not God exists. This is the proof." He shakes his stump.

"Maybe you were meant to lead a choir," I say.

"Touch it," says Doug.

I am taken aback by the offer. Then I realize I do want to touch it. The knob of flesh is smooth as a newel post.

"Thank you," says Doug. He takes his coffee in his good hand and walks away.

When I see Glinda later, I still have the sensation of Doug's stump on my fingertips.

"How do you feel, darling?" We are sitting in the little television room behind the Detox unit.

"They woke me up three times last night to monitor my heart and breathing. I guess they were afraid of convulsions. I was also taking lots of Valium to come down and apparently the Valium withdrawal is worse than the coke. Last night I was really scared."

"But you slept?"

"In between being woken up."

I am careful to say very little to Glinda about the rehab. If I say it's peaceful, I may make her want to run. I express no opinions to her about anything. I try just to listen.

"I'm going to get so fat here, Mommo. The food is so caloric. It's gross. Everybody eats candy all the time."

"There's a nice gym and pool."

"I'm not allowed to use them till I detox."

"That'll be soon."

"Not soon enough. And it's freezing. Will you send me a parka and boots?"

"Of course."

"And will you call all these people and tell them I'm sick in the hospital but don't tell them where?" She hands me a scribbled list.

"Yes."

"I love you, Mommo," Glinda says, like a baby. "I really do."

I think of Glinda when she was a baby. At five months her favorite toy was something called a Jolly Jumper. She would push off from the floor with legs that couldn't walk yet and bounce and bounce for hours. She had such exuberance and joy. Even then she was getting high.

All through her childhood, she seemed to run on sheer adrenaline. She told stories for me. She entertained everybody with her funny monologues and songs; she bewitched everyone. Then, at thirteen, she became a teenager and I seemed to lose her. There would be crises—pot, alcohol, suicide threats—then they would seem to pass. There were expensive shrinks, but they didn't seem to realize she had a drug problem. Then, at sixteen, Glinda was offered a role in a movie and she had at last found something she loved. Acting seemed to stabilize her, and I couldn't have stopped her anyway, so I let her pursue it. I was always frightened for her, but she was driven to act and she was successful. I stupidly assumed she had the drugs under control. I had become an actress at sixteen too. I thought it was normal.

"Do you know when I knew I had a problem, Mom?"

"No, tell me."

"Last summer I tried to walk through the Holland Tunnel. I was high on coke and I thought I could kill myself easily that way. But I couldn't. After that, I went to a few NA meetings, but I couldn't stick with it. I hated all the sanctimonious higher power stuff. I fell asleep in the meetings. I wasn't ready. Then when the big movie came through and I moved to L.A. it got worse. I would wake up and find myself on the beach in Malibu and not know how I got there. I would find myself wandering on the Pacific Coast Highway in the dark. It was a nightmare."

"Why didn't you tell me?" Even as I asked this, I was looking for ways not to believe it. Like all parents, I wanted to deny the truth. Then I said to myself: Shut up and listen. Just listen. If love is listening, it was my turn to listen to her no matter how guilty I felt.

"I was ashamed. Even I didn't realize how bad it was. I didn't think you'd understand. I didn't understand myself. Finally I reached a point where I wanted to die all the time. I kept thinking of ways to die. I kept deliberately overdosing. And then not dying. That was when I decided to come home."

"Glinda, you're in a safe place now. I promise you are."

"God, I hope so. I can't be trusted on the outside anymore. I know that."

"That's a lot to know."

"Are you going to stay another night?"

"I don't know what the rules are. If I can stay, I will. I have a meeting with a counselor this morning."

"They tell you it's voluntary here, but the truth is you can't leave if you want to."

I don't say anything.

"Supposedly you can get a car to the airport anytime, but that's not true. You're in the frozen tundra, the wastes of America," Glinda says.

"Glinda, remember how you always wanted me to take you to spas where there was no alcohol?"

"Yeah."

"What do you think about that?"

"I wanted you to take me away from temptation. I wanted to be safe."

"So?"

"Are you trying to say I belong here?"

"What do you think? It's not my decision, it's yours."

Glinda's counselor is called Rae-Lynn and she's short and muscular and dark. She has a weight lifter's body. Her office is full of stuffed animals and saccharine greeting cards. She is wearing a pink sweatshirt with a red heart made of glitter in the center.

"I used to be a hooker and a street junkie," she says. "If I can get sober, anybody can. Listen, I talked to Glinda early this morning and I read her intake interview from last night. Here's what she has going for her: She knows she needs help. She asked for help. Here's what's against her: Most people don't make it. The best thing you can do is look at your own relationship to substances and let her recover in her own way. We're all different. I suggest you do the family program here— if you want to. And get some support from Al-Anon."

"How do you know what Glinda's chances are?"

"I don't. Nobody knows. It's good that she asked for help. But some people are brought in against their will and recover anyway. There's no way to predict. Miracles happen. It's not in our hands. If you want reassurances, you've come to the wrong place."

Right place, wrong place, not in our hands, miracles happen. What kind of language do they speak here?

"What can I do to help?" I want to know.

"I told you. After that, you just have to let go."

"I've never let go in my life."

"Maybe that's why it's time to start."

"Can I stay another day?" I ask.

"Of course, but you won't be able to see Glinda much. You can visit with her occasionally."

"I just want to stay another night to clear my head."

"Good idea," says Rae-Lynn.

I never thought my idea of a sanctuary would be a room with a narrow cot bolted to the floor and a paper bath mat on the bathroom floor. No telephone, no TV, no radio. But I liked my room. Nobody could reach me there. Not my sisters, my parents, my husband, my friends. I could think about my life.

What had I done wrong with Glinda? When she was little and her father walked out, I decided I would be both mother and father to her. He wouldn't pay child support? Well then, fuck him. I would take care of her. And that was when I got the role of Blair the bitch on the nighttime soap opera *Blair's World* and I was making tons of money. But what I didn't realize was that Glinda needed more than money. She needed a father. A mother and nanny were not enough. I was so busy making a living, dealing with my romantic life, that I hardly had time for Glinda's life. I was forever buying her things she didn't want and didn't need.

I belong to the generation that believed children could survive anything. We got married and divorced as if we were only moving from one apartment to another. But the truth is children can't survive everything. Glinda took everything personally, suffered over everything. I should have been listening, but I was working all the time.

The character of Blair on *Blair's World* is the one that has clung to me. Blair was the original scheming bitch—a woman who married again and again and got richer with every divorce. Of course everyone thought that was true of me. In the eyes of the public I *was* Blair. Villains are always more memorable than angels, and Blair was an archvillain. She was like the queen in *Snow White*. You really believed she was capable of poisoned apples.

I never thought I was Riverside Drive's answer to Meryl Streep, but I loved being on a soap opera. It organized my life. You got to the studio early and the whole day was just crammed with work. You rehearsed in the morning and taped in the afternoon. There was no time to worry about your own life. The character you played consumed you. Blair was a thoroughgoing psychopath. She had no conscience. She never worried about the needs of others. Women loved her because she was the opposite of everything they had been taught to be. Men were intrigued by her for the same reason. Asher fell in love with me when I was playing Blair. I think he may have been disappointed when he discovered I wasn't as evil as my character. Some men need tough women to prove themselves. Asher had had a tough mother and a disappointing father. He liked the challenge of wooing me as Blair. But underneath my tough exterior I'm a softie. Like him. Was Asher disappointed to find that out? If he was, he never showed it. And I took care to hide the softie part of myself.

I borrow a parka and boots from one of the people who work at a desk near my room and I venture out into the cold again. My breath puffs white in front of me. There are soft brown pine needles on the path around the lake and my feet sink into them. The blue spruce along the path tower above my head as in a fairy tale. The frozen lake absorbs the meager sunlight into its slate surface. The ice fishermen are still out there, patiently waiting. If I were to sit in one of those little huts on the ice and put a line down into the frozen lake, would I come up with anything that might nourish me?

I am thinking of the things Rae-Lynn told me and remembering all the nights my mother came home from parties horizontal. We never thought of her as an alcoholic, but the truth is she couldn't think of how to celebrate except to get loaded. I remember a time in Paris with my family when I drank so much—at eighteen—that I went into the bathroom and lay on the floor with my cheek to the cold white tiles. I could not move my limbs. I was paralyzed. I thought nothing of this, nor did my mother, who had been in that condition many times herself, but looking back, it seemed I should have been concerned about it. My parents would have said "Nonsense!" They hated people who didn't drink. My mother looked upon a vodka martini as a magic elixir. It turned day to night, sadness to joy, storms to sunshine.

Even after her first hip surgery, she was trying to get Antonia to bring her vodka in the hospital. I had no reason to doubt that Glinda was born with the predisposition to cure her troubles with mood-altering substances. I was like that myself. What would my life be like if I stopped drinking? That day in the woods, I decide to try it. I don't tell this to Glinda when I meet her before flying home. I have signed up for the family program three weeks later and I have met again with Glinda's counselor.

"I didn't mean to imply that you were an alcoholic," Rae-Lynn says. "I just thought that you should see how all this looks to you if you don't drink. Sometimes people find it helpful. Sometimes their perspective shifts. It's your decision, of course."

"The people here are so calm," I say. "It makes you think they have something special to offer. I'd like to be calm too."

"It's yours if you want it," says Rae-Lynn.

If only it were that easy. Flying home, I realize that the whole outside world is in a conspiracy to make me drink, but I don't. It's hard not to. The pine trees and silence at the rehab make it easier. On the plane I keep thinking that just one drink will return me to that calm even though I know it isn't so. I manage to resist—God only knows how. My resistance lasts several years while Glinda solidifies her sobriety. And then I drift back into the occasional glass of wine—especially when Glinda isn't there.

———

"Where the hell are you, Mommo?" Glinda asks across the table.

"In the woods of Minnesota, years ago."

"Wasn't it beautiful? I hated Detox but then I fell in love with the place. I almost didn't want to leave when they said I could."

"I know. You were terrified to go there and terrified to leave."

"I wish we could go there now—for a retreat weekend—but there's this to think about." She taps her belly with a swollen hand.

"I love you with all my heart, Glinda."

"Me you too, Mommo."

"Let's pay the check and go buy baby clothes."

"Yessssssssssssss!" says Glinda.

We leave the restaurant and plunge into retail therapy.

Even at the worst moments between mothers and daughters, shopping is the cure-all. I love seeing Glinda looking beautiful in a new dress. There's almost nothing a new dress can't solve. Until the bill comes.

But retail therapy is hardly easy with a daughter who's already five months pregnant and getting bigger. Nothing fits as you go into the baby-growing stage of pregnancy. We all end up wearing the same tattered sacks or jeans with the fronts cut out and replaced with elastic—or leggings made for a giantess. Or various elasticized *schmattas*. Who was it who said if pregnancy was a play, you'd cut the last act? Maybe we all have. You can't sleep, can't wear anything elegant, can't fit behind the wheel of a car, and you waddle like a duck rather than glide like a princess. It seems like it will never end. Only amnesia would make any woman do it again. Though we love our children beyond all imagining, beyond all expectation. Nature is a very clever mother.

So we slide into a pricey boutique and buy baby clothes made by impoverished ladies to feed their own babies and emblazoned with labels in French and Italian, mostly bearing the names of men who would never bear babies themselves.

PART II

Winter

5

Money Is the Root

Ah, make the most of what we yet may spend,
Before we too into the Dust descend;
Dust into Dust, and under Dust to lie,
Sans Wine, sans Song, sans Singer, and—sans End!

——*The Rubaiyat of Omar Khayyam*

When I met Asher Freilich I was forty-five and living with an actor young enough to be my son. My daughter was thirteen and more grown up than my twenty-six-year-old lover. I liked to think of Nikos as a Greek American reincarnation of Colette's Chéri, but actually he was far more comfortable in the diner in Astoria where he'd grown up than he'd ever be wearing my pearls in a drawing room near the Bois de Boulogne. I had taken up with him purely for his James Dean looks and the indefatigability of his cock. Somehow, he drifted from staying overnight into never going home. But I was busy with my soap and never really had the time to properly kick him out and retrieve my spare key.

I met Asher at a theatrical AIDS benefit. Thousands of young and beautiful gay actors, and there was Asher—the silver-haired father figure. Handsome and tall with golden brown eyes, he won my heart by remembering all my movies—even some I would rather forget! He was the sort of man I never would have considered in my younger days—solidly responsible, owner of stocks and bonds and companies that did arcane things like build pipes and purify water. For someone who loved theater and movies, he had an inborn knack for business. He was a bereaved widower (before that married and divorced almost as much as me), loaded, but that was hardly what I liked about him—I who had always supported artistic losers. What I liked about him was that he reminded me of my father. They even shared the same Leo birthday—August 10—and they both had the same ferocious energy and Catskill Mountains humor. Asher was so unlike my type that I told my analyst-of-the-moment—a mountainous gray-haired woman named Bobo Bressler (née Barbara Neuwirth, who wrote sexual self-help books; *How to Be Your Own Sex Therapist* was the most famous)—that I could never be with him. She didn't buy my bullshit.

"You *can* love a man who adores you!" she said. "Just turn your head around." (I have often stolen her line when counseling friends who have met the man of their dreams and cannot see it. "Turn your head around," I say.)

Isadora felt the same way. "If you don't grab him, I will." She immediately saw that I was trying to talk myself out of a great guy.

Her advice and my analyst's proved right: Asher was funny, tender, sweet, and a compulsive gift-giver. He bought jewels as if they were chocolate truffles. He also bought chocolate truffles. These were mostly for Glinda, who adored him on sight, despised him right after I married him, and then bonded with him for life. Asher loved Glinda too. Sometimes I thought he loved her more than me.

Nikos at first tried to make a fuss about palimony, but Asher sent me to his white-shoe lawyer, Thomas Breedwell,

Esq. (I swear), who said nothing like that ever flew in New York courts. So I retrieved my key. And, astonishing myself more than anyone, I gave up my cheating out-of-work actor for a kindly billionaire. This was so out of character for me that my friends were too amused to be jealous. At least at first.

Hadn't our mothers always said, "It's as easy to marry a rich man as a poor man"? Well, it wasn't for me. Unless I was paying the bills, I felt out of control. Besides, mine was the generation that thought wearing the pants financially would give us equal rights. Hah! When I met Asher I really had to change the way I thought about men. And about myself.

But where was the worm in the apple? For a while the worm was hiding in the core. Glinda and I moved into Asher's museum-like fourteen-room duplex on Fifth Avenue. I had imagined myself transforming it from dark to light, flying back and forth to Milan with Asher and filling the place with futuristic furniture, which we would highlight with contemporary art. But Asher couldn't stand to have anything changed. His last wife—the sanctified dead one—had decorated the apartment over the years. Any change would kill her all over again.

I hated her decor. Fine French furniture from the seventeenth and eighteenth centuries, Aubusson rugs, Gobelins tapestries, vermeil cachepots and chandeliers, third-rate eighteenth-century paintings from the school of this or the school of that. Asher's late lamented wife had had more money than taste. But what could I say? Rejecting her decor was like rejecting her. She had died lingeringly of breast cancer. How could I strike another blow?

Asher was generous and loving. What he lacked in sexual technique he made up for in enthusiasm. He reveled in the daily intimacy of marriage. But was it really intimacy? After a while, living with Asher made me understand why Freud had said that not even he could analyze a beauty or a billionaire. Asher's money caused people to kiss his ass all the time, which made him both insecure and arrogant. Still, I was determined to make the marriage work. I had had enough relationships that tanked. This one was going to last.

Then there was the problem of his children.

Dickie (Richard in public) was forty and worked with his father. He didn't mistrust me nearly as much as his wife, Anita, a grasping, greedy little yenta who was sure I had married Asher only for his money. And then there was Lindsay, the lesbian daughter who could do no wrong in her father's eyes. He was always praying for a miracle and trying to marry her off. He never uttered the word *gay*. Did he think her partner, Lulu, was merely her roommate? Apparently. Lindsay was tolerable but her partner was counting on a big inheritance. Despite the fact that both kids already had generous trust funds, my appearance on the scene seemed likely to diminish everyone's patrimony.

Not that I needed Asher's money when I married him. I was writing screenplays by then and doing well. It was only when I declined into wifehood, stopped writing, and became the producer and director of our social life that the money seemed necessary. Naturally, my needs expanded to fill my husband's income. Instead of shopping at Loehmann's, I shopped at Valentino. Instead of buying caviar at Zabar's, I bought it at Petrossian. Instead of cooking for my own parties, I hired a private chef. The only thing I didn't do was hire a private secretary slash party planner. I did that myself. I had to do something besides shop.

None of this made me happier. Conspicuous consumption in New York is an ever-escalating stairway. No matter how extravagant you are, someone is more.

I understood all this from my childhood in Hollywood. None of it was real. None of it really mattered when you had three-in-the-morning insomnia and devils came up from the depths to haunt you. But for Asher it was part of the cock-measuring contest that was his life. A beautiful wife, a private jet, a duplex on Fifth, a farm in Connecticut, a house on the beach on the "East End" of Long Island, a villa in Cap Ferrat, a chef who used to work for George Soros. All this mattered because it intimidated other men and attracted women. These were symbols of dominance, which made other primates kiss your nether parts. Of course when they did, you felt both cynical and suspicious.

At the charity balls we had to go to, I would sometimes amuse myself by imagining all the participants as baboons or gibbons grooming one another, displaying reddened hind-quarters, kneeling before the most charitable billionaires and picking off (and eating) their fleas. The grooming rituals were so obvious. You couldn't really have a decent conversation anyway because you could barely hear anyone speak. But just by observing the dance of the primates you could tell who was important and who was not. The fund-raising supernumerar-ies and executive directors of charities were willing to grovel for even comparatively small change. Born on their knees, they couldn't wait to fall on their faces, and their billionaire marks knew it.

"Here comes that phony Frenchman from the museum," Asher would say. "Let's give him a run for his money." And then I would watch while Simon di Sinalunga groveled while pretending not to grovel, inviting us both for lunch, trying to set a time to come to our apartment and assess the pictures, all the while pretending to be interested only in art.

Asher loved making a monkey out of Simon, loved watching him scrutinize my cleavage in my red Valentino gown, loved watching him try to count the diamonds in my necklace. We were never more united as a couple than in public with the cameras flashing. It was our best gig. I suspected that the same was true for many of the couples at the party who flirted connubially in public, then went home and never spoke to each other— like two-year-olds in the sandbox engaged in parallel play.

Goateed Simon, marvelously turned out in a hand-tailored tux, speaking with an accent known only to museum directors and classical music announcers, went on about the new wing he was building in Central Park. Asher pretended to be fascinated.

"Are you prepared to call it the Freilich Wing?" he twitted.

"It depends," said Simon.

"How much?" asked Asher.

"It's not only a question of money."

"Then what is it a question of?"

"Can I take you to lunch in the Trustees Room?"

"Call me," said Asher, and turned away.

We were hardly out of earshot when Asher said, "That monkey says it's not about money."

"Shhh, he'll hear you."

"Vanessa, he would kiss my ass even if I insulted him to his face. Those guys have no sensitivity. They're about as sensitive as goddamned toilet seats. A human abacus with an

Italian name—that's all these guys are. You can't insult 'em. Believe me, I've tried."

Asher was a shit-disturber. Actually, that was one of my favorite things about him. He had no sacred cows. Except perhaps his late wife, who could do no wrong. Amazing how saintly spouses become after they die.

As Dickie Freilich gradually took over the everyday workings of the business, Asher decided to become an artist. Surely he had known enough artists who sought his patronage. Why couldn't he *become* one? Not for him the Sunday painting of his idol Winston Churchill nor the steel constructions of his friend Arthur Carter, he wanted to make gigantic earthworks like Robert Smithson or wrappings of man-made monuments like the Christos. What appealed to him about earthworks was how big they were, how much land had to be purchased, how many people employed in building them. It seemed that pipelines and reservoirs were not so very different from earthworks except that the earthworks had no practical use. This appealed to the cynic in Asher.

"As long as I was only building water systems I could be dismissed as a rich *grubber yung*—but when I make these things, I'm an artist! I love it! Art is defined as something useless." Asher had gotten rich in a variety of businesses from finance to real estate to water.

Asher admired more than any contemporary work Smithson's *Spiral Jetty*, built into the Great Salt Lake in Utah. We had to fly there in our plane and inspect it from all sides. We brought all the catalogs and noted the way it had changed colors over the years. Knowing of his interest in Smithson, the Dia Foundation tried to get Asher to fund the restoration of the jetty, but Asher wanted to build something as grand as

Spiral Jetty and sign his own name to it. He was sick of being a patron. He wanted to be an artist. This led him to suggest hiring Smithson as his teacher.

"He's dead," I said. "Died in a plane crash in the seventies."

"Well, we'll find another earth artist."

"Not so simple," I said. "Earth art is no longer in."

That was when he decided to take me on a tour of the stone circles of England and Ireland.

"People have always honored their gods with rocks and earth!" he said.

"But you're not honoring God, you're honoring yourself."

He looked at me critically, almost disapprovingly—like the satrap about to have the concubine killed. Then he burst into peals of laughter.

"That's why I love you, Nes, 'cause I can't put anything over on you. You know me, baby." He squeezed my hand, almost amputating a finger with the huge canary diamond I wore.

"Ow!" I yelped.

"That thing's lethal. Next time remind me to buy you a smaller one!"

I did know him. But did he know me? Did he know that I loved him with my whole heart? I wanted to make that clear.

The truth is we all want to be known. And we're simultaneously afraid of it. We want to be unmasked, and the person who can unmask us wins our respect. That was the real reason Asher fell in love with me. My knowledge of him broke through his loneliness. Maybe his sainted late wife hadn't really known him—though he'd never admit that even to himself.

Money is like sex. Sometimes the more you have the less

you have. As the Chinese sages knew, no amount of money can make people speak well of you behind your back. But Asher stockpiled money mainly to impress the other men who were stockpiling money. They were his peers, the ones he needed to impress. I'll never forget the day he learned that some contemporary of his was buying an out-of-service Concorde and planned to use it as his personal transport. It made him nearly insane.

"I know it's idiotically impractical, but it burns my ass. That bastard will get to Paris in three hours while we take six!"

"How much does it cost to run?"

"That's *not* the point!"

"And you can't fly it to California."

"I could try to get the rules bent if it were mine."

"We have a beautiful plane!" At that point it was a Gulfstream IV.

"But with a Concorde, we could have a flying palace!"

"For short people. And so what?"

"That asshole will have something no one else has."

"The Sultan of Brunei has plenty of things no one else has—including a harem."

"I didn't go to high school with the Sultan of Brunei!"

"Is that what it's about? High school?"

"You bet your bippy."

"How childish. All of life is not about high school!"

"Maybe for me it is. Besides—everything about money is childish. So what? It still buys what I need most."

"What's that?"

"Respect."

"Or duplicity. Why would you want that?"

"Everybody gets duplicity from their fellow man. I'd rather have it in comfort. My dad never learned that."

"Nobody could say you weren't comfortable. I make sure of *that*."

"That's why I love ya, kid." He kissed me on the nose.

In their own way, my parents were just as crazy about money—on a smaller scale. They had grown up during the Depression and for them the Depression was still a reality. They had transmitted that reality to their daughters. All three of us were marked by their money anxiety. All three of us felt poor despite the fact that we would probably inherit from them and had never known want or hunger or the blacking factory. In our hearts we were all Oliver Twist crying "More, please."

6

A Human Being

A human being should be able to change a diaper, plan an invasion, butcher a hog, conn a ship, design a building, write a sonnet, balance accounts, build a wall, set a bone, comfort the dying, take orders, give orders, cooperate, act alone, solve equations, analyze a new problem, pitch manure, program a computer, cook a tasty meal, fight efficiently, die gallantly. Specialization is for insects.

——Robert Heinlein, *Stranger in a Strange Land*

Winter tightens its grip. The weather gets stranger and stranger—cold one day and fiercely hot the next. There are Kansas tornados in New York and humid New York nights in Kansas. There are torrential floods in New Jersey and Connecticut. Beaches are washing away on Long Island and Cape Cod. The dunes cannot keep pace. Not even the billionaires on the East End can rebuild their sand dunes fast enough to save their multimillion-dollar "cottages."

Barrier beaches are temporary geological features—like waterfalls, like us. The whole planet seems to be washing away. Or turning to ash. We put it out of our heads as people do. "Neither the sun nor death can be looked at steadily," La Rochefoucauld said. The death of a planet might be too much to absorb, but most deaths are more specific and less apocalyptic. They start with stunning simplicity.

The doorman calls up to the apartment: "Your husband has collapsed in the lobby."

And I am in my leotard and bare feet, ready to work out with Balkan Man, my Serbian trainer.

"Gotta go!" I say to Isadora. I talk on the phone with her constantly.

"Why?" she asks.

"Asher collapsed in the lobby!"

"Oh my God! Call me back!" she orders me.

I run to the elevator as if in slow motion and slide downstairs to find my husband gray-faced and gasping on the marble floor of the lobby, muttering, "I'll be fine, got to get to the office . . ." Then he retches and falls back.

"The ambulance is coming," says the doorman.

Out in the street, it's suddenly freezing December weather. ("Ice is nice / And would suffice," Robert Frost wrote about the end of the world.) The ambulance screams up to the front of our building. Medics appear and strap Asher onto a gurney.

"I'm fine, I'll go to work," he keeps saying before passing out. The wide double doors of the ambulance gape to receive him. The medics wire him up, lay him down, and give him an aspirin. He vomits it.

"Lenox Hill," they say.

"No, New York Hospital," I protest, knowing his doctor is there. What ensues is a fierce argument with the medics, which I win.

At New York Hospital the cardiac team goes into action, but not before they check out our health insurance. I am in limbo—the limbo that always overtakes me in emergencies— free of feeling, giving orders, unhesitant, unambivalent. I always become fiercely focused whenever the life of someone I love is balanced on a wire.

Again, my husband throws up the half-dissolved aspirin. Everything is suspended like that aspirin. Death is always here in life yet willed invisible because we cannot bear it any more than we can bear news that our sun will someday go out.

Then I am in the ER being told my husband has had a mild heart attack. Then I am in the cath lab being told they were wrong about that.

"It looks like a dissecting aneurysm," says the surgeon.

"Can I get a second opinion?" I ask.

"Only if you want him dead," the surgeon says. "Time is of the essence. We must go into surgery immediately."

"But he had *breakfast*," I say, thinking of the time Glinda was three and needed surgery for a severed finger and we had to wait for her to digest her dinner.

"No time," the surgeon says, like the white rabbit in *Alice in Wonderland*.

By then, Isadora is there, translating for me. "They cannot wait," she says, "with an aneurysm."

"What's an aneurysm?"

"The wall of the blood vessel balloons out and may burst," says someone.

"It *has* burst," another voice says.

Now my husband is alert and in charge, holding an iconic clipboard.

"Sign here," a doctor says.

"Do you want a metal or a porcine valve?"

"I don't care," Asher says. "I'm not kosher."

I love him because even at a time like this, he can still make jokes.

He signs and they take him into the OR.

I realize my feet are still bare and I am wearing his huge

green loden coat over my leotard and tights. I am shivering. My feet are bluish.

Isadora is holding my hand. "It will be all right," she says. Neither of us believes it any more than we believed it when her husband came home from an avalanche in a box, his mouth twisted as if he were saying, "Shit!"

Since Isadora and I have been friends, she has gone through a series of trials that would have broken a weaker spirit. She has gone from being a wild girl to a wise woman. Since her beloved husband slammed into a tree during an avalanche, she has become the most spiritual woman I know.

Isadora is a writer who got famous way too young and then had to save herself from the brink of self-destruction. Like me, she went through terrible periods of being a love junkie and a substance abuser. But when she got clean, she was a model of sobriety like my daughter. I loved her sanity and grace. She inspired me. And despite her early fame and the criticism it brought, she went on writing. Going on is the ultimate test of character.

My daughter arrives with the clothes I must have asked her for. She has that manic humor that comes from terror:

"What does a woman wear while her husband has open heart surgery? Does she wear the J jeans and the Rykiel sweater? Or the Ralph Lauren cardigan and the Blue Cult jeans? And what about shoes? Clergerie or Blahnik? And her bag—Fendi or Hermès?"

My friend and I are laughing so as not to cry.

I grab my clothes, go to the ladies room, and get dressed

there as if I have to be properly dressed for my husband's surgery.

We wait. Doctors come in and out and we attempt to nickname them. There is Dr. Buff, with his muscled arms, six-pack, and crew cut; Dr. Dash, who runs rather than walks; and Dr. Cud, who is always chewing gum. Dr. Buff gives us a V for Victory sign. Dr. Dash says, "So far, so good." Other uniformed troops run in and out of the OR. It seems like an entire baseball team is working on my husband. It is a doubleheader.

In the last few years I have spent much of my life waiting at hospitals. First my husband's parents died nearly in tandem. Then my own parents began to fail. Once you have entered the hospital's mythic maw, your life is no longer your own—or perhaps it is too much your own. You are on hospital time, which slows to a crawl. You are at the bottom of the information totem pole. Everyone knows something but you—and if you protest you will know even less. In my family, we were always topping one another with misery. Well, now it seemed I had won.

My cell phone shrills. It's my sister Emilia—Em.

"Where are you?" she asks over the crackle.

I realize I have neglected to tell her where I am.

"Asher had an aneurysm of the aorta. I'm at New York Hospital waiting for him to come out of open heart surgery."

"Oh my God," says my sister. "I can barely hear you."

"What did she say?" I hear my other sister ask.

"She's at the hospital."

"Why?" is all I hear before the phone goes dead.

———

I am sitting beside Asher, who is sleeping in the ICU. His skin is as cold as refrigerated steak. Glinda is crying. Asher's eyelids flutter.

"Please stay," I say, touching his chilled arm. I wish I knew a *brucha*, but I have absolutely no religious education. I don't want to be a widow like my sisters. But I don't want him to live with a tattered memory either. How shall I pray and to whom? I don't believe God has a personal connection with each of us. Yes, there is what Dylan Thomas called "the force that through the green fuse drives the flower," but is it a personalized force? Who knows? It does not speak to each of us in the local language, still less in Latin, Hebrew, Greek, Hindi. I believe in God or the gods, but I'm not sure God believes in *us* anymore. Witness the Holocaust, Hurricane Katrina, the earthquake in Haiti, 9/11, and Abu Ghraib. Witness school shootings and our inability to stop them. . . .

God is disappointed in us. We failed each test. We are not kind enough or good enough to be saved. Kindness is the highest wisdom, says the Talmud. By that standard, we are not wise, we who torture our fellows and live by the labor of little dark-skinned children. There, I said it. That's what I believe. Somewhere in the universe, there must be enlightened beings, but we are not them. Slash it, bash it, tear it down like the Tower of Babel. Flood it and drown the sinners. Surely another round of evolution may produce something better than the gun-toting torturers who populate our planet.

Dr. Buff walks in and signals for me to meet him in the hall.

"Your husband has lots of *mazel*," he says. "My colleague, Dr. Ahrens, who just happened to be on yesterday, specializes in aortic repair. He did a gorgeous graft—a long one with tissue from the saphenous vein in the leg. It was an honor to watch him. Looks great. We didn't have to work on valves at all. He's a lucky man, your husband. Now all we have to hope for is no infection and good healing. No guarantees, but . . ."

"When will he wake up?"

"In a few hours."

"Why is he so cold?"

"We have to drop the body temperature for open heart surgery. We should have warned you."

You should have, I think. And yet I am immensely grateful Asher is still here—whatever his temperature. Probably it's a blessing I knew so little about aneurysms yesterday. If I had known the mortality rates, the narrow window of time in which to get help—I would have done exactly what I did. Instinct had proved as good a guide as knowledge.

"Mommo—he's freezing," my daughter says, having tuned out the doctor's explanation. She begins to tremble. She grabs my hand and squeezes it.

"Will you hate me if I wait in the hall?" Glinda asks.

"Of course not—you can wait wherever," I say.

Isadora hugs me. Glinda flees.

From then on I spend the days and the nights in the hospital. In between, I'm forever on the telephone listening to useless advice from friends or reciting chapter and verse of Asher's condition to his relatives. People pretend to care when you are about to become a widow. In New York they proffer massage therapists, shrinks, acupuncturists, plastic surgeons. As if you could jump up and reconstruct your life in an instant. As if you'd *want* to.

I am clear enough to know that if Ash doesn't pull through, it will take me years to get used to the idea. I won't be out looking for love in all the wrong places. Nor will I be placing ads on the Internet. How do I know this? I just know. I know because I have a best friend who lost her husband to an avalanche at fifty and took nearly a decade to open her arms and mind to love again. You can't just replace people like T-shirts or sneakers. I've begun to understand that if I lose Asher, my whole life will be stunted. I never realized how much I need him, how much I love him.

Am I crazy, or do I hear an undercurrent of exultation in the voices of acquaintances? The phone seems to whisper: *Glad it's not me, glad it's not me, glad it's not me.*

Every night at midnight, Asher's brother calls me from L.A.

"What did the doctor say?"

"Nothing much."

"He can't have said nothing much."

"They never commit themselves—you know that."

"How is Ash?"

"He has no idea what we've been through. He was out of it the whole time. He tells me the aneurysm was mine, not his. He wants me to get him Chinese food."

"And what do you do?"

"Get him Chinese food."

"How can you do that?" my aged brother-in-law yells. "He should be on a low-fat diet."

"Then come here and put him on it. He won't eat anything but Chinese food for me."

"Are you kidding?"

"Absolutely not. You know how stubborn he is."

"But make him eat healthy food. His life depends on it."

"I'm trying."

And it's true. Isadora and I go to Whole Foods and buy everything low fat—beans, rice, fish. Asher will have none of it—nor hospital food.

"If I don't know how long I've got to live, I'm going to eat what I like," he says. And with that he drowns his Lobster Cantonese with several packets of soy sauce.

"Not salty enough?"

"Damn right."

I try to talk to him about what he remembers from his surgery.

"I remember nothing. I was flying."

"Do you know you were out for three days?"

"How would I remember that? But I do know you saved my life. And I know how much I love you."

"Me you too." I reach out to put my hand over his heart but the bandages stop me. He grabs and gently squeezes my hand.

We had both been in the same physical space but we each had inhabited a different mental space. There seemed to be no way to share what we'd been through. The paradox of illness. Whose reality is real? The sick inhabit one universe, the well another. They may not even be parallel. The branes between them are thicker than forged steel.

Asher is fearless. I sit by his bedside, watching him read the paper as if nothing has happened.

"I can't believe how calm you are."

"Because I slept through the whole crisis. You were awake."

"Were you ever afraid you were going to die?"

"No. I knew it was going to be okay."

This was the reason I had married Ash. He was brave where I was fearful, calm where I was crazed. Natural Prozac ran in his veins. He was an optimist. Optimism was the source of his success. He would have been an optimist in Auschwitz. And he would have survived. I don't know about me.

When (after 9/11) I sat at my computer surfing for bomb shelters to install under the country house (despite the fact it has no basement and perches on solid rock), he reassured me that it was *not* the end of the world.

"It's not even the *beginning* of the end of the world," he said.

You had to love a man like that. I did.

It was a winter when it snowed and snowed. The city was re-peatedly blanketed in snow. Trees came down. Power went out. There was more salt in New York City than in the Dead Sea. Climate change was upon us—or El Niño or both. The snow fell endlessly as if to bury its own ghosts. I kept think-ing of the Joyce story "The Dead" to remember how he de-scribed "the snow falling faintly . . . like the descent of their last end, upon all the living and the dead." There was an end-of-the-world feeling to this weather.

One day, after a powerful snowstorm that buried cars and reminded me of the great snow of 1947 when I was a tiny child. (My parents had come back to New York for meetings, brought all three of us, and we got trapped by the blizzard.) I put on my warmest clothes and boots and go walking in Central Park with my beloved poodle, Belinda.

The trees are weighted down with snow. From time to time a great glob of snow falls from a snowy branch. The city is silenced. Kids are running around wearing bright-colored parkas and pulling sleds. I keep seeing men who look like my father—until they turn around and I realize their faces are different.

The descent of our last end—how much nearer we are to it than Joyce was. He lived in a world without nukes, without climate change—and still he suffered over his daughter. No human life passes without disappointment and suffering. No children without trouble. He invented a new language to tell his troubles. Don't we all wish we could?

I once had an acting teacher who used to quote Stanislavsky at the crinkle of a script. "Never lose yourself while acting," he used to say. "It all comes out of your own being." At first I had no idea what he meant. I had thought acting was becoming another person—but in truth it was becoming more actively yourself—more human. This took forever to understand.

But here in the snow, it makes sense. Who am I really? A stumbling human being, age unknown, who knows she's going to die. I never really believed it before.

I walk up Pilgrim Hill and lie on my back below the snow-laden statue of the pilgrim with Belinda—who loves snow. I raise my arms and press them into the snow as I did with my father when I was little. When I stand up, I see my angelic imprint, a bit puffy from my parka, arrayed around me. My dog's angelic imprint is also blurred.

"Always go to sleep hungry," I can hear my father saying. "That's the secret to staying slim—no night eating." What he didn't say was that he believed slimness guaranteed immortality. Boy, was he wrong.

―――――

When you're young your energy is so abundant that you think you can do anything, but it's also unchanneled. As you get older you have to channel your energy because it's limited.

Wet snow keeps cascading from branches in explosions of white. As I walk with Ms. B., I grow frightened that a branch will fall on my head and kill me. Danger brings excitement, Stanislavsky also said.

I keep thinking I see my father darting behind trees. He looks just like he did when he and I were young. Do I believe that if I grow young again I will have my handsome father again? What is magic after all—but the deep intention to change? What is magic but turning back time?

As I walk home in the snow with Belinda, I think about how impossible it is to explain to the young what happens when you know you're not immune from death. Everything changes. You look at the world differently. When you're young, you have no perspective. You think life lasts forever—days and months and years stretching out to infinity. You think you don't have to choose. You think you can waste time doing drugs and alcohol. You think time will always be on your side.

But time, once your friend, becomes your enemy. It gallops by as you get older. Holidays come faster and faster. Years fly off the calendar as in old movies. All you long for is to go back and do it all over, correct the mistakes, make everything right. My father must feel that way. I understand when it is too late to tell him.

Does everyone die with unfinished business? What about

those gurus who choose the hour of their deaths, call in their students, and say good-bye? Or is that just a pleasant myth?

Being young is not just about looks or sex. It's about energy. I amaze myself by having such sudden abundant energy that Belinda and I jog all the way home in the slush.

7

Loving Mr. Bones

Death is a shadow that always follows the body.

——Proverb

Have you ever spent your days shuttling between one hospital and another? That was what my life became. My father was in the hospital again. He bounced in and out of the hospital as people do at the end of their lives. He was at Mount Sinai, my husband at New York Hospital—and I the flying shuttlecock between them, propelled by love and fear.

When I wasn't running between patients, I roamed cyberspace lonely as a cloud. I was searching for love online, where the Internet shimmered with possibility. Here, for example, was a chap who wanted to fly his lover around the world in a private plane. He had read *Emmanuelle* and thought that plane sex was the height of eroticism. I played the game for a while, sexting my plane fantasies in response to his. I was sure there was a place of ecstasy and transcendence I could find if only I knew the code, if I only knew the key word. It was a place of sacred streams, healing waters, plants I could eat to gain immortality, and endless perfect lovers. I had to traverse a magic wood, full of whispering leaves and swaying shadowy trees.

I knew it existed, but just as I discovered the entrance, it would vanish behind the trembling foliage. If only I could enter it, I'd be free of despair, of aging, erasing my history and starting all over again. The Internet was a sort of fountain of youth, a potion I could drink to let me rejuvenate and reinvent myself. I had registered at Zipless.com as if I could change my life by rewriting my story for prospective online lovers. I was supremely in control—as long as I never met any of these imaginary swains and was never disappointed.

Currently, I was also corresponding with a "Byron" who claimed that he had lived his life in accord with poetic principles—whatever that meant. "Rite on my loverz bods," he texted. That didn't seem promising. Was the Internet a vast sea of lunacy? Sometimes it seemed that way. And sea levels were rising!

"Do you still think Zipless is a fraud?" I ask Isadora the next time we have lunch.

"Aside from the fact that they stole my title?"

"Yes. You should sue."

"I don't want to spend the rest of my life in a lawsuit. When Zipless first appeared, I was incredibly pissed off about the theft of the title, but I thought the site might be great. Now, like most of the Internet, I find it gross and misleading. I don't believe you'd ever find the perfect lover there."

"Why?" I ask.

"Because if people can be anonymous they tend to lie and cheat. As a writer, I take responsibility for what I say. I sign my real name. On the Internet people hide and usually when people can hide the truth eludes them."

"So you've stopped believing in Ziplessness."

"Absolutely," Isadora says. "It works in fantasy, not in reality. In reality you have to trust someone to have great sex, and how can you trust what you read on the Internet? The Internet has fractured our attention span, made headlines more important than explanation. How often have I followed a headline only to discover it told me nothing? It stimulates our eyeballs, not our brains. So often, I click on a story only to be disappointed. I don't even like tweets if people don't use their real names. Isn't it ironic that people think of me only in that context?"

"Just as people think of me as Blair," I say. "We are all stuck in old news."

At the hospital, my father was hanging on in the ICU. He seemed happy to see me, but he was intubated again, so he couldn't speak.

The nurse reported that he had pulled out all his tubes the night before and had to be reconnected by the morning shift. He even pulled out the feeding peg.

I sat by his bedside watching him doze and wake and cursed myself for what we were doing to him. We were not observing his living will. It was too hard to interpret. Nobody dared to play God. Nobody dared to make a decision. Perhaps my hysterical older sister was right. We should let him go. But how? Who could make that grave a decision?

Asher and I were both incredible news junkies. We watched it all with fascination and horror. Little kids left legless after stumbling on cluster bombs, hospitals overflowing with people killed in marketplaces, in schools, in cars (just for turning the ignition key). This was the world we'd made. Yet letting go of a ninety-three-year-old father had not gotten any easier.

All my life there had been war. And what had it accomplished? Inflated the price of oil and Halliburton stock and killed the brown-skinned children. The younger the children, the more they died. And the women died. And the youngest men.

When I thought about the legless children, I couldn't sleep. How could anyone sleep?

Well, my father could. At least if he was sufficiently drugged. He had been an athlete once and now he was Mr. Bones. You could see his hips and pelvis through his coverlet. His legs were skeletal. He weighed less than one hundred pounds.

What can you wish for as you watch a beloved parent struggling against the end? Should you wish for death, or life? And how much do your wishes matter?

The lucky ones die in restaurants after a good dinner. Or die in their sleep in bed during an erotic dream about a lover long since passed to the other side. I hope to merit such a death.

The tall, skinny geriatrician from the palliative care team strides in.

"Mr. Wonderman," he says to my father, "I'm your doctor. How are you feeling?"

My father pulls out his tube with great élan and croaks, *"Malpractice!"*

"Dad, you really know how to get along with doctors!" I say.

"Let me out of here!" he mutters, trying to scream. He's undoing the tubes, detaching himself from the IVs and the peg and trying to stand up. He's very shaky but he almost manages. The male nurse arrives.

"If you put that tube back in, I'll kill you!" says my father.

Standing there, I am proud and terrified at the same time. I take the doctor aside.

"Leave the tube out. If he dies, he dies," I whisper. "Don't torture him."

"Okay," the geriatrician agrees. But my father refuses to get back in bed. He doesn't want to be here. Who can blame him?

"If I promise not to put back the tube, will you settle down?" the doctor asks.

"I don't know," my father croaks. But the nurse comforts him and somehow gets him back in bed without tubes and monitors.

"I want to go home! Home!"

So we start to make plans to bring him home.

It's not an easy proposition. We need to rent a hospital bed, hire a nurse, get morphine prescriptions filled. But, having gotten his way, my father seems to have made an astounding recovery. He is hoarsely yelling at everyone, ordering the palliative care team around, and they seem cowed.

"What is palliative care? It's how you turf the old out on the ice floe! You're the Angel of Death team, that's what you are."

In my heart, I'm cheering him on.

"Take me back to Eleven West!" he shouts. That's the

swanky-hotel floor of the hospital, where they overcharge you to death.

My sisters return and we accomplish the transfer out of the ICU and to the hotel floor. My father is triumphant. He's talking and breathing and screaming like a champ. His old strength seems to have returned. He is coasting on the propellant of anger.

"You know what Mark Twain said?"

"What?" I ask.

" 'Reports of my death have been greatly exaggerated!' "

"You know what Art Buchwald said?" I ask.

"No," mumbles Daddy.

"I don't either, but he *refused* to die."

"Refused!" screams my father. "Refused!"

How this happened, I don't know, but even in his parlous condition, my father has made a special friend at the hospital. He's a geriatric psychiatrist named Dr. Cragswell, first name Fin for Finnegan. He has a long braid down his back and iron-rimmed spectacles like an anarchist from the early twentieth century, and he thoroughly disapproves of the ministrations of the palliative care team. He has taken me aside several times to tell me that he thinks my father has "an acute but not fatal illness."

"He's playing to you, Ness," my younger sister says. "He's a star-fucker."

"He's crazy," my hysterical older sister says. "We love crazies because we're so crazy ourselves."

But he seems to be able to reach my father when no one else can. For this, I'm grateful.

"If you take your father home, I'll come see him," Dr. Crags-well says.

"Thanks," I say.

My sisters ignore him.

They think he's *playing* to me. They think being an actor protects you!

Hah. It *exposes* you rather than protects you. Everyone butts in. You spend your life surrounded by buttinskies. For three and a half decades I have been the actor the world hailed or hated. That certainly brings the kibitzers in. And the crazies.

The nurses tuck my father into bed and admonish him not to get up again. They dress the wound from where he pulled out the tubes, the peg. The nurses are all so gentle—especially the male nurses. They gentle my dad. He responds to their caresses.

The sun is going down and the sky has that neon blue color that tugs at the heart because it's so fleeting. *L'heure bleue.* I stay a little longer and then run to the other hospital to see my husband. I'm so exhausted that I fall into a deep sleep on the reclining chair in my husband's room.

Now it's midnight. The park has been snow-frosted all of January and February so there are icy patches on the walkways and a crust of frozen snow over the hills. The snow seems blue in places, black in places. A gibbous moon lights the treetops. The streetlights leave puddles of blue on the snow.

A procession of very old people in hospital gowns, some leaning on walkers, some on canes, some in wheelchairs rolling along by hand, appears. My father and the tall thin doctor with a long braid down his back lead them. My father has a staff he has made from a stout fallen branch. Dr. Cragswell has a scythe. The scene looks like an Ingmar Bergman movie filmed in New York.

My father is exhorting the old people to move along, not to give up, to disinherit their ungrateful children. His voice is scratchy and faint but I can almost hear him from where I watch.

At first, the procession consists of only a few people, but now my father has put down his staff and he's drumming on a snare drum he wears on a strap around his neck. *Mamapapamamapapa* it goes—as he used to say when he tried to teach me to play the drums. (My high school dates always loved coming to my house because of the full set of timpani.)

And with his drumming, the procession gets longer and longer. He seems jubilant. He has triumphed. All the ancient people are following him over the snowy hills of the park. As they follow him, they get younger and younger. The bent straighten up and throw away their walkers. The wheelchair rollers sprint out of their wheelchairs. My father has become the Pied Piper of the Park.

"I never realized how much the old resent the young," I tell my father in the dream.

"Of course we do!" he shouts. "If we could be young again, we'd know what to do! What did you *think?*"

"I thought you loved us!"

"That's secondary!" he shouts. "We got here before you!" I try to shout at him, shout my shock and disappointment, but I wake myself up.

———

"You certainly are a noisy sleeper," Asher says.

"I have a great deal to be noisy about. That was a crazy dream."

"Tell me."

"You know dreams—fascinating to the dreamer, boring to everybody else. I don't want to bore you."

"What do you remember?"

"My father in the park, leading a procession of dying ancient people over the snow."

But even as I describe the images from the dream, they waft away like smoke in the wind.

"We have no rituals for death," I say. "That's why it's so hard. We're supposed to disappear when we're no longer young. Our parents make us uncomfortable because they remind us of our fate. And we make them uncomfortable because we remind them of what they've lost. We need new rituals, new philosophies. If only we *believed*."

"In what?"

"That's the problem. How can you believe in God after the Holocaust, the Vietnam war, Iraq, Afghanistan?"

The question lingers in the air like the smoke of my dream. My husband invites me into his hospital bed. He hugs me. Weakly.

"But why can't you enjoy what we have now and forget about the future? The future doesn't really exist. All we have is this moment."

"I know."

"If I die, I don't want you to wear mourning for the rest of your life like Queen Victoria. I want you to live. I want to *liberate* you to live. You liberated me."

"I know."

"For most of my life, I had no idea how to live. Now I do. Because of you. I want to give back what you gave me."

"I know," I say. Asher has a vulnerable side he reveals to me that nobody else ever sees.

"You know but you don't know at all."

"I know."

He hugs me very tight.

I try to go back to sleep and reenter the dream. I want to hold on to the vision of my father stomping through the snow. But it is gone.

My husband is getting better as my father is getting worse. Asher is still in the hospital, but he is talking to his pals on the phone. He has shortened his aortic aneurysm to "a heart attack" for their sake. No point in going into long discussions of open heart surgery and grafts. His buddies are shaken up enough by his absence. They depend on him. And he depends on them. Talking to them on the phone makes him feel useful again.

I want to feel useful too. I start taking notes on what is going on. I don't want to write a memoir, but I am sucked into the immediate life-and-death crisis. Isadora had suggested this as catharsis. I am willing to try.

Now I am keeping notes on my father and my husband. I realize how alike they both are and how much I have depended on men to complete my life. Once, I'd had an idea for a movie in which a woman revisits all the old lovers in her life and they all turn out to be the same man. Is that my story? Is that every woman's story?

———

In my notebook I try to imagine climbing the mountains inside my husband's head. If love is empathy—I want to be him,
become him.

Asher never remembers his dreams—nor will he this
one, in which he glides down over the Green Mountains,
slightly bumping the anvil-shaped thunderclouds, climbing
again as if on a giant eye. Is this heaven? It might as well
be—a green strip between two mountains with biplanes, tri-
planes, monoplanes, and slivery gliders studding the verdancy
of a lush Vermont summer. But heaven is not ready for him
yet because the next thing that happens is a gust of wind
that lifts the wings of his Cessna 210—his very first plane
when he was in his twenties—and whirls him up into a ther-
mal over the mountains. His flaps will not deploy, so he
knows he cannot land. He keeps whirling like a leaf in a
storm. He is trying to undo his seat belt, but it is stuck. His
headset is issuing only deafening static.

I know what to do, he thinks. I'll wake up rather than
crash.

He wakes to find himself intubated with lines leading
away from his penis. He can't remember how he got here or
why.

A hospital, he thinks. An aortic aneurysm. What are the
stats? One in ten survives? The stats must be better now,
mustn't they? Maybe this is heaven? Or hell? I'll know when
I meet my father and mother. If I see them, I'll know it's one
of the two. But it must be hell because I can't speak. Or
maybe heaven because of the clouds. Then sleep overtakes
me again. My mother and father are reduced to the size of
Ken and Barbie dolls I can hold in my hand. They are dressed

as if for a Palm Beach function. My father in a Turnbull &
Asser tux with a scarlet bow tie and cummerbund, my mother in Angel Sanchez midnight blue chiffon and all her em-
eralds and diamonds. They are carrying party hats and
tooters as if it's New Year's Eve at the country club. But what
year? Am I eighteen or thirty-six or sixty? I must be dead
because I know Palm Beach is hell.

Or are we in the Hamptons at some ridiculous screening
or benefit? The carefully fixed and lacquered Sally
Smerdykaf drifts into view holding a clipboard full of boldface names. I'd rather be dead than in a place where you
have to dress up at the beach. My idea of heaven is Vermont—
with its country inns, its horse farms, its grassy landing
strips, its old hippies making pottery and growing pot. Hippies who march down Main Street on the Fourth of July
wearing battered tricorns over their long gray hair and down-
at-the-heel Birkies on their gnarled old feet. The scent of
cannabis drifts down—though we no longer partake.

We got married there. I remember saying: *Harei! At me-
kudeshet li, b'tabaat zo k'dat Moshe v'Yisrae.* Behold! You
are married to me with this ring according to the laws of
Moses and Israel.

A justice of the peace did the legal stuff. Our friends and
family were there by the pond. Both sets of parents alive and
looking relieved that we'd finally found each other—as if it
always was *bashert* and they knew it but wouldn't tell.

You couldn't tell the bride's family from the groom's.
They were all one breed. And cousin Ira taking bets on how
long it would last. We were such bad marriage risks. Both
of us bouncing off walls through our twenties, thirties, and
most of our forties—our similarities sealed the deal. Plighted

our troth. Sex inevitable, not easy at first because of fear of having everything and losing everything. And then— giggling in bed, multiple orgasms—and omelets, old jokes, and Yiddishkeit. What bonds two people? What makes two one? Pheromones? Brains? Genes? Nerves? You gotta have nerve, moxie, and chutzpah, and nothing is ever guaranteed. All your nerves know before your brain and your nose. How else do you know? And you keep knowing.

She would say—Do that one more time and I'm leaving. And he would say: Where would you go? And she would laugh. No place to go when you've bonded like that. Every year you get more bonded. Crazy Glue.

I know he loves me. Even his unconscious loves me. I never had that before. And that's what most people who meet Asher can't see. They buy his tough-guy act. I don't. I see the sweet boy underneath the bluster. I imagine him bluffing his way through his Bar Mitzvah. I see how vulnerable he is—saw it even before he got sick. I see the way he looks at me—as if his eyes could pierce my skin. I know he even loves me in his dreams. And I want to love him back that way. Can I?

"What do you think of this all-female house?" my mother asks. That is the only reference she makes to my father's hospitalization. She lies in bed, wearing diapers, waking and sleeping, attended by rotating nurses. When I look for a vase for the flowers I've brought her, I discover that every container is veiled by greasy dust—something she never would have allowed when she was awake and aware. All the women in my family are mad housewives, compulsive cleaners. Veils of grease are not our style. This is the way the world ends, I think, greasy dust covers all.

I give her a big smooch and sit by her side in her wheelchair while she fades in and out of consciousness.

She wakes up, sees the flowers by her bedside, and says, "I should paint them." But the truth is she hasn't painted in years. She has forgotten how.

My mother tilts her head back and looks up at the ceiling with her mouth open as if she would swallow the sky. This is no life for the energetic person she once was. If she could see herself, she wouldn't be happy.

When babies spend their days waking and sleeping, we're not sad because we know their lives are going forward. But an old person's slipping in and out of sleep is only a warm-up for extinction. We know it. Do they know it? And if they know, do they care?

Yes!

What on earth are we going to do with our old, old, old, very old parents? If we have to choose between babies and old people, we know damn well what we ought to do. My mother always used to tell the story about the mother eagle that could save only one of her baby eaglets from a catastrophic storm that threatened to blow away their nest. So she asked each eaglet what he or she would do when she was old and utterly dependent on his or her care. The first eaglet answered: "Stay and take care of you, Mother, for the rest of your life." The second said: "Sacrifice everything for your welfare, Mother." The third said: "I will have eaglets of my own to care for, and they must come before you. If I can save them and save you, I will do it. But if I must choose, I will choose *them* when you are old." Of course the third eaglet was the one she saved.

Survival of the tribe is always more important than survival of the dying. Triage was my mother's lesson to us. It was
far less ambiguous than a so-called "living will." Yet how to
follow it? We'd better harden our hearts as the earth becomes
overrun with the dying. The old are rigid. They don't want to
give up their power. Unless we replace them with flexible new
people, we have no chance of changing the world. I assume
that's why the immortals invented death. They must have
known that immortality was no bargain.

Remember Tithonus—the man who could not die?

Remember Tennyson?

The woods decay, the woods decay and fall,
The vapours weep their burthen to the ground,
Man comes and tills the field and lies beneath,
And after many a summer dies the swan.
Me only cruel immortality
Consumes: I wither slowly in thine arms,
Here at the quiet limit of the world,
A white-hair'd shadow roaming like a dream

Tithonus asked Eos, goddess of dawn, for immortality, but
he forgot to ask for the eternal youth the gods enjoy (if they
do). The gods are tricky. Probably out of boredom. It must be
boring to live forever. You must be very specific in your wishes
or they'll come back to haunt you. Eos went her merry way,
rising always in her pink-and-red chiffon with streaks of gold
and blue; Tithonus lived out his immortality as a decrepit,
walking, talking corpse. But at least he talked poetry.

My father wished for more. Immortality and eternal youth.
Of course he got neither.

Aldous Huxley, who was prophetic about so many things—from artificial insemination to artificial wombs to euthanasia—envisioned the dying wafting to the next world on a cloud of music and "soma." Pain would be obsolete, drugs ubiquitous. We're almost there.

I like morphine as much as the next addict. I'd break my leg again to have it, I sometimes think. Byron and Shelley lived—and died—on laudanum, tincture of opium. Who could blame them?

You don't really become aware of the body until its beautiful balance breaks down. My father couldn't eat, couldn't swallow, couldn't pee, yet wouldn't die.

If only I could get inside his head and know what he was thinking. But I couldn't even do that when he was well. He was always running away—to the airport, to the baby grand, to the drums, to the Metropolitan Opera, to Carnegie Hall, to the office, to Japan or Italy or China. He was an escape artist. And so, of course, was I. It took me years to find a marriage I didn't want to escape from, and yet I kept having escape fantasies. Perhaps it was the escape fantasies that led me *not* to escape. Perhaps fantasy is the only way marriage endures, or life.

Now my dad could not escape except by dying. I wondered if he knew that. Of course I didn't have the courage to put the question to him. All I could do was hold his bony hand, then go to the other hospital and dream of his escape through the park.

Of course, when he finally died, our mother was in the other room. We'd brought him home to a hospital bed, our pockets full of morphine and syringes that were never used. We settled him in bed, made him comfortable, and my sisters left.

"Where is La Seconda?" he asked. (That was me.)

"Here," I said.

Some sixth sense prevented me from leaving. For several hours he was very peaceful, watching. I was watching him watching. Then he seemed to drift off. At one in the morning he awakened in pain. He made a terrible grimace and with difficulty took in three enormous gulps of air. Were there three angels summoning him as kabbalistic tradition tells us? Was he resisting their pull? Or had he lost the strength to resist?

It seemed he had been waiting to come home. He had been looking at the snowy hills of the park, imagining his escape. And now he was gone. The transit from life to death rode on the breath.

"Is he in that box?" my mother asked at the funeral.

"No," I said, without lying. He was already far away.

When identifying his body, I kissed him on the cheek, leaving my lipstick valentine, but his expression was no longer his. How quickly the spirit flees!

"I love you, Dad," I said to the cold cheek.

I might as well have been speaking to a hollow doll. Without animation and warmth, without movement, the flesh is almost unrecognizable. What remains is in the survivors' memories: mirroring, imitated gestures, words, music.

I was wearing a black dress with silver jewelry, and one of my earrings must have fallen into his coffin. I didn't even feel it drop—or see it glimmer. Only when I got home that night did I realize it was gone. I was glad it was spirited away by what was left of him—along with that print of my lipstick on his dead flesh.

Inevitably, as with all my nonobservant dead relatives, we

had to rely on rent-a-rabbi. My father never belonged to a synagogue. He refused to belong to any club that would have him as a member (à la Groucho Marx). His mixture of insecurity and arrogance prevented him from being a joiner.

His will dictated that each of us should speak about him at his funeral. And we did. We would have done it without the will. It was his anxiety that made him put it in the will. Remarkably, for three such different daughters, we all stressed the same things. Music was in all our memories. He played the piano through our dreams (his baby grand was good to him, as Billy Joel sings. She may have been the only woman he ever completely loved). He dragged us to concerts and operas until we understood. He would not let us close our ears.

When we buried him, we sang. I will always see us there in the snow, singing in quavering voices, "I gave my love a cherry that had no stone, I gave my love a chicken that had no bone, I gave my love a baby with no cryin . . ." It was as if we were standing around the piano in the old West Side apartment. We sang as we shoveled the snowy earth over his casket.

The bones clatter, but music covers all. His whole life was music to our ears—if not his own.

And the strangest thing is this: When he was alive, I thought all our conversations were partial, frustrating—unintelligible. But once he was dead, we really began to talk. We talked through all my dreams. We talked every night till the small hours of the morning. Alive, he was closed and careful. Dead, he told me everything. I think he may be dictating to me now.

8

Grief, Loss, Ex-wives, Dogs

I touch on grief and loss like one touching electricity
with his bare hands, and yet I do not die. I cannot
grasp how this miracle works. Maybe once I finish
writing this novel, I will try to understand. Not now.
It is too early.

—David Grossman, "Writing in the Dark"

You can go from the country of the well to the country of the sick in a split second. I have become a sleepwatcher. Asher has been kidnapped by the god with the wings in his hair.

"Did I fall asleep?" he asks.

"I guess so."

"I hate this," he says. "I don't want to make you a slave to my illness the way my father made my mother."

"It's a little soon to worry about that. You've scarcely been here a week."

"My feet feel all pins and needles. Will you walk me around to see if they'll support me?"

And we slowly set out down the hall of the cardiac unit, pushing his drips and tubes on a wheeling stand. He is at least a foot taller and sixty pounds heavier than me, but he leans on my shoulder as if I were twice his size. Step by step we go, stopping only to close the back of his hospital gown so he won't moon the staff.

"How are the pins and needles?"

"Not as bad as last time. But now I want to go back." He is huffing and puffing and glad to sit on the edge of the bed when we get back to his room.

"God, I hate this," he says. "How can you stand it?"

"Don't worry about me. This is nothing. You're the one who returned from the dead. Lucky you—my dad did not."

"But he was ninety-three," Asher said, not adding anything about his own age.

We both came back from death in different ways. We are putting one foot in front of the other, learning how to walk again.

The parade of ex-wives begins.

Asher's ex-wives are a tribute to his lifelong love affair with his mother. His mother was a six-foot beauty married to a five-foot mogul; all of Ash's wives were tall but me.

First comes Diane, a redheaded television producer who married a goyish trillionaire after leaving Asher. She won her original fame from her documentary on dominatrices in Vegas, but now she does crime shows, sci-fi shows, and reality shows. Diane struts in on four-inch platform spikes, wearing a skintight black leather pantsuit, her red ringlets curling around her face, her eyelashes beaded with black. She has a ski-jump nose, courtesy of Dr. Nasebery (I swear that is his real name), and implanted D-cup breasts.

"I couldn't believe it, Ash, when I heard. You were always so strong—didja have it *forever*, darlin'? What did they say? Why didn't they catch it sooner?"

She totally ignores me. She perches on Asher's hospital bed and begins running her fingers through his hair, holding his hand, displacing his tubes; she seems entirely ready to jump under the covers, even in her lethal-looking spikes.

I know that Diane left Asher before his big success to marry someone "really rich rich," as she puts it, so I decide to take a walk down the hall and leave them to their reminiscences. If she needs to act as if she never left him, so be it. Her self-delusion has nothing to do with me. But no sooner have I circled the unit twice than I feel compelled to return. Now Diane is regaling Ash with tales of her difficulties raising money for her next show—a reality show about psychiatrists— and I see the ulterior motive in all her cuddling.

Can there be anything ruder than a rant about television financing at somebody's sickbed?

"Can't we talk about this when he's better?" I ask Diane.

"Oh—I'm so sorry. I didn't mean to be inconsiderate, but you know how obsessive I am about my work—please forgive. What an idiot I am!"

I nod but she isn't looking.

"I'm gonna besiege you with healing energy!" she exclaims to Asher, extracting a little brown bottle of lavender and sage oil from her huge alligator handbag and handing it to him. "I'm gonna be here every day, I promise." I know it's probably the last time we'll see her.

"How did you ever marry anyone so dumb?" I ask when she's left.

"I was young," Ash says. "I knew it was a mistake from the beginning. When we were on our honeymoon in London, I wandered out one night and picked up a hooker—just to prove that I was still free."

"Did she ever know?"

"God, no. She would have been furious."

"How did you *feel?*"

"As if I wasn't hers hook, line, and sinker. Forgive the pun. I needed to know that then. She was so controlling. I stopped fucking her almost from the first month we were married. What did I know about myself then? Nothing. I hadn't been analyzed. I was very primitive. I fought control with control. I stopped even *liking* her." He fingers the bottle of aromatic oil. "Healing energy! What a crock! Go sprinkle it on someone else!"

"There's a guy down the hall who looks like he might need it. Poor slob. I still can't believe you *married* her."

"She didn't really dress that way until *My Personal Slave* made her a celebrity. She's sort of a lapsed good girl. Not like Lola—who was a lapsed bad girl practicing on me."

"What'd *she* look like?"

"Another tall redhead like my mother."

"'And where is she *now?*'—as my old analyst used to say."

"God only knows."

But God must have known more than She let on because Lola saunters in about an hour later.

She's become a judge—a television judge called Judge Lola. But Asher doesn't know that because he never watches TV. She is still wearing her white shirt and jabot—which, on TV, peeks out from under her black bathrobe.

She speaks in an obviously exaggerated Nu-Yawk accent to show she's one of the people. And she has very big auburn hair.

"I can't believe you've never seen me on TV."

Asher throws up his hands and laughs. "You think it would be good for my heart?"

"I most certainly do!" Pronounced: *Eye most soitenlee dew!* "It would do you good!"

"Lovely to see you, Lola."

"Don't lovely-Lola me. I just came because I thought you might be dying. You seem okay, so I can delay our reunion."

"You never know, I could go at any moment."

"Nah—you're too tough. If you came to my television court, I'd read you the riot act."

"So read it to me now."

"I can't endanger a patient. Even I have some manners."

"Your manners were always perfection."

"Thanks to Viola Wolf and her lessons on manners, I always knew which fork to use." Viola Wolf was *the* manners coach for New York kids in the fifties.

"And you got all the forks too, not to mention the spoons and knives," he says.

"So buy your own," she says, looking at me.

"We eat with our hands," I say. "More fun that way." Actually, Asher and I had both lost most of our silver to divorce, but now that our parents were going, it was starting to accumulate again—unmatched sets. But who cares anymore? Anyway, unmatching is the latest trend.

"I'll come back tomorrow," Lola says, flouncing off. But she never comes again either—which is a blessing.

"We should have a party for all your ex-wives," I suggest.

"What do you think this is?"

"A preview of your funeral?"

"The best thing is—I won't be there."

"How do you know?"

"I don't, but I'm hoping the Hindus are wrong about reincarnation. Enough is enough."

"You'll probably outlive me by decades."

"I hope not—especially when I see how lousy my taste in women was except for you."

As if is this is her cue, Leona walks in.

She is tall, thin, fixed, lifted, and implanted, and again, her hair is auburn. Leona is a few years older than Asher. They have remained friends and are in touch, so I know her and rather like her. She is my favorite ex-wife. She makes herself comfortable and begins to tell us about her protests against the Iraq war. She has become a Quaker. I think I should become one too. Quakers are the only ones, it seems, who believe in anonymous charity. They give to the needy and sick without putting their names on buildings. I like that. They're also antiwar without wanting to be congratulated for it. Modesty is an endangered virtue in our society, and they have it. I admire that.

Yet war has always been with us—and somehow we survive. It's the war on our planet and our uncertainty of the planet's survival that pains most. When Louise Bogan, one of my favorite poets, averred "more things move / Than blood in the heart," she was comforted by the survival of nature. But maybe we've come to the end of nature. Even our children may not survive. Or our grandchildren. Unthinkable.

We have trouble with death. We think it's un-American. We think it won't catch us. Not for us the screaming and wailing, the tearing of hair, the wearing of sackcloth and ashes. These things are thought to be "self-indulgent"—a word favored by those who most manifest it. But what *is* self-indulgent? What does it mean? Does it mean indulging the self to prevent its being extinguished? Does it mean holding on to one's personhood when in danger of being swept away, being swept into impersonal eternity? If so, then we *should* indulge our screams and wails. We should give ourselves space to indulge our mourning for the individual. Whatever eternity may offer, my hunch is it won't offer individuality. Maybe this is good. Maybe individuality is pain, but let's at least mourn it when we give it up.

I am thinking such thoughts when I come home to our apartment at midnight that night to find twenty-seven messages on voice mail and seventy in e-mail, many from zipless .com. I can't deal with any of them. I am too tired. Ziplessness does not even make my heart flutter. Then suddenly I see an e-mail titled "The Wit and Wisdom of Isadora Wing." There's a quote intended especially for me: "Sex without love is a cancerous cigarette we willingly smoke." I burst into laughter. What a wily friend Isadora is! She has always told me she's going to collect her wit and wisdom in a little book—and here she is giving me a taste. I shut the computer down, still giggling.

Belinda Barkawitz, my big black standard poodle, leapt onto the bed with me and began licking my face. How would we face troubles without our dogs? Tired as I was, and even though she had already been walked by that New York necessity, the dog walker, I pulled her pink hooded sweater over her fluffy head, leashed her, grabbed my coat, and went downstairs to walk her. All the dog people were out—the walkers, the owners, the trainers. New York becomes a village when you have a dog. Looking down, you recognize the dogs before you recognize their human companions. I used to laugh at people who disdained the word "pet," but now I sympathized with them. In fact, instead of using the politically correct term "animal companions," I thought the canines were the gurus and we merely their disciples. This was the proper hierarchy if hierarchy there must be. They were so much more humane than we, in all the qualities that matter most— empathy, loyalty, sense of smell. The nose is the most primal and infallible organ. If only we all lived according to our noses, the world would be an altered place.

Belinda frolicked and skipped. She wanted to cheer me up. She knew immediately what I needed and was delighted to offer it. Like all poodles, she was psychic.

We met a schnauzer she knew but she gave him only a minimal sniff, turning all her attention on me. Then we met two golden retrievers and their owner, who had an identical hangdog expression.

We met a white-haired lady with a blind rescued grey-hound, a gray standard poodle, and a springer spaniel.

"How is Belinda?" she asked. "Have you got her Addison's disease under control?"

"Pretty much. How's Horatio?"

"He's doing well on the prednisone and Percorten."

"Belinda too. And what about Tiresias?"

"You'd never know he was blind unless I told you."

I nodded enthusiastically and petted the blind greyhound, who nuzzled me while Belinda repressed her jealousy. The springer pulled to go home. It was cold and the wind was up.

"Night," I said.

"Night," said the lady. "Shall we get them together for a dog-date?"

"Absolutely."

I took her phone number and gave her mine, thinking that

in New York, dogs could provide you with whatever you needed in the way of comfort.

We walked home, rode the elevator up, and made weather conversation with the elevator man, who persisted in calling Belinda Melinda. So what? If Belinda didn't mind, why should I?

I'm having lunch with Isadora Wing and trying to evoke for her how crazy all my meetings with the Zipless guys have been.

"He was a sweet-faced blond of perhaps forty. And when I opened the door of his apartment—with a key provided by the doorman—I found him growling and crawling at my feet."

"What did you do?" asks Isadora.

" 'Hi,' I said sweetly. 'I love dogs.' But that was the wrong response. He apparently wanted to be whipped.

" 'I don't really believe in whipping dogs,' I said. 'Not even when they're naughty?' he asked. And with that he peed copiously on the floor. I opened the door and left as fast as I could."

Isadora laughs hysterically. "You mean you've never met a man who wanted to be a dog before? I've met plenty."

We pause and sip from the water glasses on the table, rinsing away remnants of the smiles pulling at our mouths and marking each one with our own shade of lipstick. Then Isadora gets more serious. "You are taking terrible risks by meeting strangers," she says. "You don't even understand the danger you're in."

"Okay" I say. "I'll be careful."

Then I tell her I just received a provocative e-mail from

someone at Zipless, and that I'm intrigued: "I want to be your personal slave," it read.

"I don't even understand what a personal slave is," I say.

"I know," says Isadora. "They're people who have been trained by dominatrices to do your all your dirty work for nothing. Some people—particularly powerful men—find that attractive."

"How do you know all of these things?" I ask my friend.

"Research," she says. Then she adds, "Years ago, I used to be invited to a party given by a famous dominatrix in New York who was desperate for me to use her in my books. There I saw famous heads of companies wearing aprons and doing the dishes. At first, I couldn't believe it. I had no idea why they needed this humiliation. And they even paid the dominatrix for the privilege. Apparently, men who humiliate others need to be humiliated themselves. The human heart is a dark, dark forest, and you never know when you're going to wander into something you can't get out of. I would recommend that you don't take chances. What I've discovered is that men are more confused by all the changes of our society than women are, and you never know how they are going to react."

"I can just imagine myself trotting down the street with my personal slave on a leash," I say.

"Don't," Isadora says. "You have no idea how much trouble a personal slave can cause. They're sort of like the oompa loompas in *Charlie and the Chocolate Factory*; once you turn them on, you can't turn them off. They swarm all over and bring their friends. You have no idea. What you have to do now is recognize how lucky you are. Treasure Asher while he's here. He's your soul mate. The last thing you need is a personal slave."

If only I could have taken Isadora's advice then and there, but I was too edgy, too curious, too afraid of dying.

I do meet the man who bills himself as a personal slave, but I'm happy to say I bring my friend Isadora along for protection.

"What exactly does your slavery consist of?" I ask the applicant.

"I do whatever you need—from housecleaning to sex to shopping. And I am happy to do it for both of you since you seem to be together. Nothing is too much. It's my pleasure to serve you and all those you instruct me to. I will wear whatever uniforms you need me to, work whatever hours, never ask for a thing in return. I will wear rocks in my shoes for penance if you need me to, sleep in the kitchen behind the garbage, peel potatoes and live on the raw skins . . ."

Isadora and I begin to giggle, at which the slave seems terribly hurt.

"Don't make fun of me!" he shouts. "It's not kind to make fun of another's obsessions! I may have a disease, but I can make your life heaven if only you let me!" And he begins to cry.

Isadora apologizes for our insensitivity, begs his pardon, tells him we respect his illness—and, putting her arm around my shoulder, hustles me out of the coffee shop where we'd met him.

When we're more than a block away, she says, "Do you believe me now?"

"Yes, yes, yes," I say. "You're right. I'll never doubt you again."

"When it comes to perverts," she says, "please don't doubt I know my stuff. I've done it all and find it boring by now. What are friends for but to rescue you from your craziest fantasies? Your husband needs you. I understand that even if you don't. You're just afraid he'll die and leave you alone. That's the source of your panic. But perverts won't solve it. I can promise you that."

"So you never had fun in your crazy salad days? Never?"

Isadora looks off into space, searching her memory. She's quietly breathing.

"Tell me!" I demand.

"Well, there was one time in Paris with a woman known only as the Countess. She had many personal slaves."

"And?"

"I was fascinated with her and asked if I could attend what she called a *ceremonie*. No spectators, she said—only participants—and I'm not sure you're ready. Well, that really piqued my curiosity. The Countess was very old and famous for her beautiful dungeons and gorgeous slaves. It took months. Finally, I persuaded her. Don't make me tell you this, it won't be helpful to you at this point in your life."

"Tell me!" I say.

"Well, her minions told me what to wear, where to go, and when I arrived wearing black velvet, a full mask, no panties, very *Story of* O, they insisted on changing all my attire anyway. I was led through many dark corridors till I was dizzy with desire and fear. Eventually I was laid down on a velvet altar, where a gorgeous young man—her personal slave—performed cunnilingus till I was exhausted. The Countess directed him while she pierced my skin with tiny silver pins. She had various male slaves who bathed me, fucked me, sang to me. It was incredibly erotic, and it's nearly impossible to describe—like most ecstasy. Part of the pleasure was my loss of control. I did not tell anyone what to do—the Countess did. Except for the pins, she made love to me only with her eyes. I had given her complete control and I trusted her completely. How many hours and how many orgasms I do not know. But it was exciting beyond anything—and I've never been able to talk about it except now, to you."

"Why was it so special?" I ask.

"I'm sure it was being totally out of control. Politically incorrect it may be, but we all respond to giving up our will. If it's not *our* will, we can't feel guilt or ambivalence. We turn ourselves over to another. Some people get that from being chained or bound. But giving over the will is extremely erotic. I wouldn't dare write this, but I know it's true. We are such strange creatures in our sexuality. Every time I think I know everything I find I know nothing. Most people are utterly unsubtle about sex—but the Countess knew it took total surrender. When the night was over, I wept in her arms and couldn't stop. Have you ever surrendered completely?"

"I don't know," I say.

"Well, now is not the time. You have too much else to do. You have Glinda, your parents, and you have Ash. But someday in the future, maybe we'll visit the Countess. You're not done yet. The future still gleams ahead of us."

"What an amazing friend you are," I say. "But tell me, why would you never write about it?"

"I think sex has to be utterly secret or it is utterly misunderstood. If I wrote what I told you, I would be asked dumb questions like, 'So every woman wants to be dominated?' Or 'What does this mean for feminism?' It's not about anything political. In our private lives we live our fantasies and even our fantasies change. What works at one time in our lives may not work in another. It's impossible to generalize about sexuality—even one's own. The only way to keep it pure is to keep it unspoken. Keep it out of words. Words are not where sexuality lives. Without privacy, there is no ecstasy—which leaves out the Internet, the press. I learned that the hard way."

I just sit there staring at her in amazement. Isadora is the only person I know with whom I could have such a conversation.

9

Age Rage

I am too long in the tooth to think you can make demands on life and expect that they will be granted, like waving a magic fairy wand.

——Annie Lennox

Ash came home and at first he was very weak. He lay in bed, complaining about lying in bed. He entertained his brother, his competitors, various artists he admired. He even entertained me. He had not the least interest in sex. He was probably afraid it would kill him. I worried about that myself.

No matter what the cheerleading gurus of aging may say, sex among seniors is not what it once was when we were young. Viagra is not for everyone. It gives many people blue polka dots on the retina. It makes others faint. Shots and pumps are unaesthetic.

At least we were alive and together. How dare we ask for more? We had beaten terrible odds and we were still holding hands in bed.

I look around at my friends and I see a world of widows— or almost widows. If I were more entrepreneurial, I would set

up a sex shop for widows—someplace they could come, get
their needs swiftly taken care of by young studs, and then
move on to their grandparently duties, professional duties, fil-
ial duties (all their mothers are old-old as opposed to oldish).
The rules of *old* keep changing. We used to think sixty was
old. Now it's the prime of life. But does that mean people
want to admit to it? My widow sex shop might not work because the widows would sabotage themselves by falling in love
with the studs—the way Isadora nearly fell in love with the
personal slaves in Paris. Their hearts would break. Someone
would sue, the secret would be out, and the shop would
be closed down. It would get into all the papers.

I did not want to be a widow. I was too young to be a
widow. At sixty pretending to be fifty, the world was full of
unattached women rattling around, looking for a place to put
all that unfulfilled sexual energy.

Asher was calm. Denial served him well. He never thought
he might die. He simply did as he was told by his doctors. He
didn't argue, didn't think apocalyptic thoughts. He was so
much saner than I was.

Getting older means giving things up—sex and good looks
in particular—but Ash never complained. And he always
thought he'd get better. I loved him for his optimism. Hadn't
Dashiell Hammett said, "You got to look on the bright side,
even if there ain't one"? Asher might have said that if he were
a hard-boiled writer instead of a hard-boiled billionaire with
a soft center.

"I don't want to be a widow," I say to Isadora on the phone.

"Who does?" she asks.

"And I have the fear I'll never encounter an erection again."

"Ah—'the old in-out,' as Anthony Burgess called it. Possibly overrated. Be patient. There are a million different ways to have sex. I've already told you that. Maybe you need to think about why you have such a need to hold on to control."

"Are you blaming me?" I ask her.

"Absolutely not," Isadora says. "I would just say you are only looking at sex in a very narrow way—as if it were a form of deep-tissue massage. It can be much more. Re-lax. Re-fucking-lax. You are not in control of the universe."

What was wrong with my generation of women? We thought we would get better and better forever. We thought war and disease would afflict only people on the other side of the world. Even after 9/11—which was said to have changed everything—we still believed we had charmed lives somehow and that there was nothing Botox couldn't fix. We should have been preparing for global warming, armageddon, and the loss of our loved ones, but were we? Not at all. We were focusing on surfaces as usual. What would it take to wake people up to the danger we all were in?

Often I thought of myself living at the top of a crumbling flooded skyscraper at ninety. Little boats would be steaming around the towers, trying to save the last stragglers, but I would refuse. Before my tower crumbled, I would jump into the waves and slowly sink. Why would I want to go on living in a world like that?

Ash called out to me from the bedroom.

"I just wanted to see your face."

"What do you need?"

"Just you."

"Why are you so cheerful?"

"Here's how I figure it," he said. "I had a weak spot in my aorta and it ballooned. They put in a much tougher fabric—which should be good for decades. Besides, what earthly good would it do to worry?"

"That's true. But I worry if I don't worry."

"That's because you use worry superstitiously—as if it could keep the wild elephants away."

"You mean it *doesn't?*"

We both laughed and hugged. What on earth would I do without him?

"Oh God—that hurts."

"What?"

He pulled up his pajama leg and there was huge red swelling on his thigh, where they had taken a vein for a graft. Under the incision, there appeared to be pus.

"That looks horrible," I said. "People get the worst infections in hospitals. You could have staph or MRSA. I'm calling the doctor."

"Don't be ridiculous. It's nothing."

"It is most certainly *not* nothing."

He tried to temporize, to talk me out of it, to talk the doctor out of it, but over the course of a week, it got worse and worse.

A week later, we were back in the hospital, having his leg looked at.

"Clearly an abscess," the doctor said. He opened the flaps of the wound and greenish yellow stuff came oozing out. I looked into the wound; saw the white cells and fluid and ooze, which seemed to me like the primordial matter itself. Dizzi-

ness came over me. To my horror, my knees buckled and I
slipped down to the floor. When I came to, Asher had gotten
a penicillin shot and his gash had been drained and dressed.

"That was the first time I ever fainted," I said. "I must really
love you a lot. There's nothing like a gaping wound to show
the fragility of flesh."

"Only you would think of it that way," he said.

We didn't even try to make love for weeks. Ash was taking all kinds of medication to lower his blood pressure and he
was exhausted. But when we did, it was clear there was a
problem. Modern medicine had a name for it: ED. Fortunately, modern medicine also had a cure for it: Viagra. The
problem was Viagra gave Asher those infamous blue spots, a
blurriness that convinced him he was going blind, and the
feeling of having been run over by a truck.

"There's always the pump," I said, having been briefed on
this stuff by female friends.

"What's the pump?"

" 'Watch your penis grow to amazing size with the senso-
sensational, silky pleasure pump in blow-up or electronic
mode.' "

"That sounds horrible."

"I'm told it can be sexy."

"It sounds dangerous to me. Like it would make my penis
fall off."

"There are other things—you can ask your urologist."

So we began the quest for an erection fixer to fix the erec-
tionless fix we were in.

Clearly we were not the only ones in this situation. The
pharmacopeia contained an endless variety of answers—from
injections to implants, from rings to pistol pumps. We were

the generation that never gave up. Orgasm was in our bill of rights.

I began my online research for sex toys. Not only were there pumps, vibrators, rings, wands, and slithery gels, but there were also environmentalists warning about the dangers of sex toys. Apparently they contained toxic substances. Apparently they were unregulated. Apparently there was a muckraking tome to be written about the dangerous objects people put inside—or outside—their bodies. They leaked gasses. They disintegrated with soap and water, with bodily fluids. No federal agency was testing them. And yet they sold by the millions. Nobody seemed to care about the dangers—except a few killjoy environmentalists.

But Asher found none of these toys the least bit erotic. The dildos were so big they made him feel small. The pumps seemed dangerous. The rings likewise. Maybe he was still too tired to contemplate any of this. There had to be another way.

When we did try to make love, it was clear we were not on our way to holding hands in two side-by-side bathtubs as in that ad for erection boosters. Every channel was full of ads for them. The metaphors were weird: The street falling away and becoming lush wilderness. A couple going up in a multicolored hot-air balloon. A beautiful English girl in the Caribbean reassuring her "honey." An old couple harvesting cucumbers. And then that absurd image of the lovers holding hands in separate old-fashioned bathtubs. What madman thought that up? We were just lying there and looking at a limp dick.

Until your spouse nearly dies, you never really believe in your own mortality. Until you give up sex, you never believe you are old. Now I believed I was old, and I didn't like it. I didn't like the hairs on my chin. I didn't like dyeing my eyebrows. I wanted my youth back—even with all its miseries. I envy the young and they don't even know they are enviable. *I* certainly didn't know it when I was young.

I hate, hate, *hate* getting older. I would sell my soul to the devil to stay young. And then an idea begins to dawn—for a play.

I am in a rage against age. To that end, I have recruited dermatologists, yoga teachers, exercise coaches, nutritionists, herbalists, physical therapists, and doctors—alternative and plain.

There is no shortage of antiaging specialists in New York—from dermatologists who harvest and reuse your own fat to those who freeze your facial muscles with toxins. There are blasters and scrapers, injectors and fat-suckers. There are skin resurfacers, fraxelists if not taxidermists, pore shrinkers and redness faders for rosacea sufferers. There are plastic surgeons and acupuncturists and even hypnotists who regress you into false youth you dream is real. But I want more. I want magic.

While Ash was slowly mending, an older actor friend of mine hit town. We had been flirting for decades both on set and off. Heeding Isadora's advice from lunch the other day, I reasoned that seeing him would be less risky than a Zipless stranger but promising enough to excite me. I was just scared enough of the future to meet him at his hotel—a brand-new boutique-y place way downtown.

He was the kind of leading man who played James Bond when he was young but now played evil Borgia popes. He was

English, RADA-trained, and handsome in a semi-spooky way—hollow cheekbones, deep-set green eyes, shaggy brows, and sonorous voice. He often joked that if he got much older, he'd eventually be cast as Nosferatu.

"I'm finally going to play an ancient vampire," he said, embracing me at the doorway of his suite.

"Am I supposed to say mazel tov?" I asked.

"I think you're supposed to hold up a cross," he said. "To protect yourself."

I knew he had always fancied me and he knew I had always fancied him. One knows these things. Of course, we were both married—to other people—which always helps.

His name was Nigel Cavendish, and we had done a season of Shakespeare a million years ago.

We reminisced together in his suite. Both not drinking a drop due to our membership in various twelve-step programs.

Then we began to kiss good-bye and good-bye turned into hello and he swigged from an open bottle of Amarone his producer had sent and I got drunk on the fumes. Before we knew it we were both half undressed on the floor and stroking each other's aging skin tenderly.

"Shall we repair to the bedroom?" he asked, indicating it with his handsome hairy head (quite silver by now). And I nodded, and before we knew it, we were on if not *in* the queen- (or king-) size *letto matrimoniale*.

"I've always wanted you," he said.

"Me too," I said.

And I nodded but said nothing more because we were kissing so deeply. And soon he was sucking my nipples and touching my cunt. Then he was licking it enthusiastically. And then he was unrolling a condom onto his beautiful cock—by which time it seemed rather late to object.

"Shall we?" he asked in a most gentlemanly fashion. But, not waiting for my ladylike answer, he began to enter me.

It seemed we made the beast with two backs for hours and hours and hours. We muttered and murmured and kissed and hugged and licked each other wherever our tongues could reach—but neither of us seemed to be getting close to a climax. Neither of us could relax. Neither of us could re-fucking-lax. We both needed to be in control.

"I seem to see my good lady wife, Vivienne, floating through the wall," he confessed.

"Banish her," I said, not able to banish Ash. I could never banish Asher. He was in my bones.

Nigel and I were valiant at sliding and stroking and tweaking and making loving nibbles. But nothing seemed about to happen. No wave crested, no sunrise rose, no jagged lightning pierced the place where our bodies conjoined.

"I promised Vivienne I'd never do this again," Nigel said. "And she's arriving tomorrow."

"Don't worry," I whispered.

"I don't want to leave you high and dry," he murmured.

"Don't worry," I said again. "The timing's not right. We're both worried about other things."

"Perhaps next time we meet?" he asked.

"Of course," I said. "Of course." Women of my generation lie as easily as we kiss.

Later, we sat in the living room of his suite, nibbling caviar and pâté. He drank more Amarone. I drank mineral water.

"Are we still friends?" he asked.

"Loving friends," I said. "We'll have our time."

But I knew we wouldn't have our time, because we just weren't bonded in that particular way. Not every couple can turn into loving lovers—no matter how much they think they ought to be. The stars have to align a certain way. Worry has to be banished. Wives cannot drift through walls and husbands cannot be home recovering from hearts that attacked them. Many conjunctions have to conjoin for a good conjunction. I had known that before, but somehow I had forgotten. Being with Nigel only made me miss Ash more and more! Strange how I had to be with Nigel to realize how bonded I was to Ash. I was so lucky not to have been caught in my various experiments.

Later that night, I had a dream in which I found myself thirty years younger as if by magic. I was with Nigel. We were both between marriages and we were wholly open to each other as we hadn't been when we'd met earlier that day. Our romantic lives were before us, not behind us. Because aging is not only about flesh—it's also about our great expectations when we are young.

And that was when I began writing the play. While Asher recuperated, I plunged into a fantasy born of my rage at aging. In it, a woman who is furious at the passage of years finds a way, she thinks, to reverse them. I plunged into research for my play. I read everything that included magical transformations. I saw movies. I read magical spells in *grimoires*.

My play began with two friends of a certain age—Isadora and I?— at a table on a bare stage:

"Don't you want to be young again?"

"Are you kidding? I'd sell my soul for it."

Maybe I could even convince Isadora to work on it with me? It would be fun to collaborate with a real writer.

"I dream of being young again," my character says.

"Me too," the Isadora character says.

"All I want is to be thirty years younger, knowing what I know now."

"I'm there. So how do we do it? Spells? Potions? Magical thinking?"

"Do you know any real witches who can do it?"

"No such possibility exists. I've looked."

"I wonder about that."

"Because when we *were* young, we didn't appreciate our youth. That's what makes me *nuts*!"

"We didn't know the power we had—or how to use it."

"True. Too true."

"So you used to know all these wiccans. Do you still have the phone numbers? They probably use e-mail now—wicca .com."

"Well, *find* them. Or I will."

The idea was to tell the story of a woman getting younger by means of witchcraft.

My heroine was visited by a man who claimed to be Mephistopheles. He could be played by my friend Nigel. He claimed to be able to grant her "the wish that dare not speak its name." It was of course the wish to grow younger, the Faustian wish of all Faustian wishes.

So I invented these wiccan characters out of a Halloween pageant—two possibly gay warlocks and an ancient female witch—who came to tempt my heroine with dreams of re-versing age. *And* she fell for it—even signing away her soul in blood. Miraculously, she became young again. Or did she only *believe* she had?

I'd never written a play before, but I really got into it, filling it with all my campiest fantasies of magic and time travel. My warlocks wore long capes and had elaborate body piercings. My ancient witch dressed like Lady Gaga on steroids.

I had very little idea of what I was doing. But maybe I had some beginner's luck. The dialogue began to flow.

"How much do you want it and how much are you willing to pay?" Meph asks.

"What sort of payment?" asks my heroine.

"We'll get to that later," says Meph. "What is magic but the deep intent to change?"

"Time," my heroine says, "was once my friend. Now it streams by faster and faster."

"So how much do you want to stop it?" asks Meph.

And so it went. I was having fun playing on the page—something new for me. I totally let go and allowed fantasy to take over. Isadora told me that every book she had written was a complete self-analysis. I began to understand what she meant. Fantasy can lead you to reality, but you have to be open.

As I saw my heroine transformed, I worried about the dues she'd have to pay. Her soul? Her child or grandchild? I went on clattering over the keys with panic pounding in my chest.

Meanwhile, my phone kept beeping with new potential lovers on the line. I had long, flirtatious talks with some of them, phone sex with some of them, but illness, death, and my play kept interrupting. My play had got me by the scruff of the neck. It was teaching me a new kind of freedom. Besides—I didn't think I wanted the distraction of Zipless anymore. Asher's illness had thrown me because I had taken his love so for granted.

Who were my fictitious witches and what did they mean? Never ask that of yourself while writing. It may stop you cold. Just trust that if *you* believe in your characters, others will too. I learned that the hard way. Whenever I thought too critically about my work, I couldn't write. Isadora had said that too.

In most Faustian transformations, the dabbler in magic is punished. We're not supposed to play with time and the devil. Challenging the gods shows a lack of humility that often proves fatal.

I thought I was just fooling around with an old story. Why then did I feel so scared?

What I didn't know then was that for anyone who writes, a story is not just a story. It's also an amulet. As someone who had spent my life mostly speaking other people's words, I was innocent about that. Oh, I had written made-up screenplays, but never had I written a story that came from my own soul.

Gradually, it dawned on me that I was trifling with matters of life and death. I made copious notes on how to end this play. Beginnings are easy but endings are hard. Was it a comedy or a tragedy? Was my heroine really given another chance at youth—or was she deceived by her own fantasies? Was the tone to be satirical or sad—or a mix of the two? While I pondered these things, I planned a long trip to India with Asher. He probably wanted to go because he thought he was dying and it would be his last trip. India strikes everyone differently, but many of us associate it with Hindu ideas of reincarnation.

Isadora and I are on the phone again. I'm in my apartment and she's in hers. Belinda Barkawitz is sick and I don't want to leave her.

Vanessa:
I'm writing a play and you're not writing anymore. What's going on here—this is nuts!

Isadora:
Well, I have something to tell you. I haven't told anyone and I didn't want to talk to anyone about it because I was afraid to jinx it. I've been writing fantasies.

Vanessa:
What do you mean by fantasies?

Isadora:
I have no idea what I mean. My characters go to these other planets. They discover Goldilocks planets. They get away from our poisoned earth and create utopias on these virgin worlds. They get away from the Koch brothers and evil companies trying to destroy the earth and instead of Goldilocks planets being so far away, they are suddenly near enough for us to populate them with humans. But there is a fine-tuned selection process. The chosen people have to be kind, love the environment, dogs, trees, flowers, . . . especially dogs! Especially poodles!

Vanessa:
I think it's wonderful that you're writing, but do you really think you can screen people? And only have good people on the spaceship?

Isadora:
I said it was *fantasy*.

Vanessa:

Well, it certainly sounds like fantasy to me 'cause
we know it's impossible to screen for the good
people. . . . It sounds impossible to me.

Isadora:

It's probably impossible but I told you these were
utopian fictions. I really don't know where I am
going with this. I'm scared to death because it's not
what I'm known for. I'm known for writing honestly
about women and sex . . . blah, blah, blah—and
I'm sick to death of it!

Vanessa:

I can certainly understand that—one does get sick
of whatever one is known for. It's typecasting—who
doesn't get sick of it? We all get sick of it! They
kept wanting me to play Blair the bitch over and over
again. It made me ill! I wanted to play King Lear as
a woman and nobody would finance it. I wanted to play
Macbeth as a woman with Lady Macbeth being the man
and nobody would finance it. I wanted to do a female
Hamlet, do you remember that?

Isadora:

(Laughs).

Vanessa:

And do you remember the time I tried to get a movie
made of one of your books?

Isadora:

Which one was that?

Vanessa:

Oh, you know the one. It was set in ancient Rome.
I think it was called *Livia* and was about Hadrian's
wife. You remember . . . he had a wife named Livia
who had an amazing villa with murals of birds and
flowers. The frescos are in one of the municipal
museums in Rome. They're unbelievably beautiful. But
nobody wanted to finance a movie about Livia. They
kept telling me it should be about Hadrian because he
was the emperor, and who would give a shit about his

wife? Although she was brilliant and beautiful and
a force in Rome at the time—but nobody wanted to
finance a movie about a *woman*!

Isadora:
Yeah, I vaguely remember. That was a while ago!

Vanessa:
So, I do get it. . . . You've been writing these
fantasies and have told nobody. Who's the heroine?

Isadora:
Heroine? Hero? Who cares? We're human beings. Some of
us are ruled by what happens below the belt and
some of us are not, but we're ambivalent, stumbling,
grumbling human beings. Far too smart for our fragile
bodies. Far too clever for our mortality. So I
basically wanted to imagine genderless people smart
enough to know that they would eventually die and act
accordingly.

Vanessa:
Would you let me see some of these pages?

Isadora:
Absolutely not. I'm just writing them for myself.
They're not for publication. They're not for reading
by friends.

Vanessa:
Darling, just think about it. . . .

Isadora:
I'm thinking. . . .

10

Old Dogs

In order to really enjoy a dog, one doesn't merely try to train him to be semi-human. The point of it is to open oneself to the possibility of becoming partly a dog.

——Edward Hoagland

And then my dog, Belinda, died.

Belinda is old. Old is the problem with dogs. Love 'em and lose 'em. One morning, she refuses to get up. She lies, unable to move, panting, her nose dry and her eyes tearing big gray gloppy tears. I carry her downstairs and take her by cab to the animal clinic.

Most of the humans waiting with their boxes and leashes and doggy strollers are middle-aged women. Only a few men. Boxes chirp and mew, dogs drool and sniff. Occasionally a snake lifts its head out of a box as if we already were in India—or the Garden of Eden.

We get attached. We project our fears and wishes onto our animal companions.

"Max, sit down," says a blonde with Band-Aids all over her face.

The kids are gone but dogs linger on. Dogs as incontinent as old ladies, dogs with moles, dogs with wheels instead of legs. As I wait for Belinda to have a chest X-ray and various blood tests, I watch the whole range of human-animal inter-action. Women convinced cats are their babies, or wounded birds or lame dogs with flopping rear paws.

I wait and wait. I read every animal magazine. I drink a sweet coffee concoction out of a vending machine. Eventually a vet comes out and talks to me as if I am three.

"Belinda is not doing well for an older poodle. She is in crisis—probably because of her Addison's, but has a fever of a hundred and six and crackle on one lobe of one lung. We may need to keep her overnight. Would you be good enough to go to the cashier?"

What I am I going to say? Keep my sick dog for free?

Of course, I take my credit card to the cashier. After they ring me up for thousands, I am invited to visit Belinda in the doggy ICU. She seems dead till she looks up at me with her big questioning eyes.

Then they take her away for more tests and I am invited to leave her overnight yet again.

We named her Belinda Barkawitz because she was a happy barker—a big black standard poodle who spun around in circles, making her joy audible. Everyone loved her—strangers on the street, dog people, cat people, people who loved no one.

Because dogs live only a short time, they represent passages in our lives. Belinda came to us when I was in my fifties and she saw me through many losses. She was smart and gentle, as loving as a rescued mutt and as joyous as a jumpy baby bichon. When I visited her in the ICU on subsequent days, she always perked up at the sound of my voice.

I had always admired standard poodles but I'd never had one as my companion. Belinda was my first. When I met her,

I kept asking her, "Are you my dog?" And she kept barking happily—which I took as a yes.

She had a routine at night. She fell asleep in my office, then made her way onto our bed at three in the morning. We woke up with her furry sighing at our feet. She was a daily lesson in living one day at a time. Anticipation and regret were not in her lexicon. We wanted nothing more than to be like her. Live in the moment, we tell ourselves. But only our dogs fully practice that. They are our Zen masters. We want to emulate them but rarely achieve it fully.

I made the mistake of allowing the vets to remove a tumor from Belinda's flank. The tumor was benign but the operation was the beginning of the end. In trying to save my beautiful Belinda, I may have hastened her demise. I may never forgive myself, but I know she forgives me.

She was the most extraordinary bitch. Hair black as the moonless night sky, eyes brown as milkless chocolate—or indeed "olives of endless age," and little hairy feet with ebony nails that clicked when she pranced on poodle paws. Belinda Barkawitz was joyous and free.

The breeder had called her Bella, but we preferred Belinda—an eighteenth-century name from "The Rape of the Lock" by Alexander Pope.

Now lap-dogs give themselves the rousing shake,
And sleepless lovers, just at twelve, awake:
Thrice rung the bell, the slipper knock'd the ground,
And the press'd watch return'd a silver sound.
Belinda still her downy pillow press'd,
Her guardian sylph prolong'd the balmy rest:

'Twas he had summon'd to her silent bed
The morning dream that hover'd o'er her head

On the bone-shaped silver tag we purchased for her collar we inscribed: "I take care of Vanessa and Asher. 'Pray tell me sir, whose dog are you?'" So we knew she was a witty bitch, well versed in English literature. Like me, she was without a BA or an AB but no less clever for all that. Like my Russian grandfather, she was an autodidact.

I knew I was in love because the first time she barfed on me in the car, I was as entirely unbothered as if I'd given birth to her. Vomit is vomit but a beloved child's vomit might as well be your own.

She was of noble poodle pedigree, but like many aristocrats, she was inbred and suffered a genetic flaw. Had she been a rescued mutt, she would have been hardier. Instead, like JFK, she suffered from Addison's disease. It meant that her adrenal glands ceased to function when she was only five. Or was it six? We loved her the more for that because she required more care. Oh, we knew we were besotted, but we were not ashamed. We were in love. Love knows no shame. Does it really mean never having to say you're sorry?

She was dearly predictable—her bed, the floor, our bed at three A.M. I often awoke at seven to her philosophical doggy sighs. She rarely farted. But her sighs were profound.

And if she farted, we found the complexity of the scent another sign of her humanity. She loved not only biscuits but bagels, smoked salmon, and chopped liver. Yiddishkeit was her middle name. She was a Jewish poodle, a *Jewdle*, you might say. But not shrewish, totally sweet and kind. She loved even yappy small dogs. And kids.

We didn't love her because of the admiring glances she evoked on the streets of New York. No. We loved her for her intuition and her conversational skills. She knew us. Deeply. And believed we knew her.

Virginia Woolf claims in *Orlando* that dogs have no conversation. I dispute this. Belinda's conversations were infinitely wittier than most of the mots you hear at charitable benefits—those unique forms of torture New York City society so favors.

Why must we parade our charity in public when true charity is anonymous? The people who give and give yet refuse to put their names on buildings are my heroes.

As for the conversations to be had among self-celebrating philanthropists—inaudible mostly. No one can hear a word over the false compliments and the clinking of glasses. And if one could, their platitudes would stimulate little thought— unlike Belinda's sighs.

Her sighs plumbed depths we could not measure. Her sighs were conversation of the truest sort, for they told of smells and tastes and gopher holes and deer. And what can be better conversation than that?

Nature is the best conversationalist of all.

Unlike male dogs we'd had, she didn't stray. She knew enough to stay where she was safe. And yet what is safety among mortal creatures? Does it even exist?

I leave you to ponder this. We pass this way swiftly and but once—or twice. Who knows? Perhaps the Hindus are right and we are born again and again in different forms. I am sure that I was once a dog—which is why I have such an excellent sense of smell and such empathy for canines. I can tell immediately whether a perfume is based in roses or jasmine and a moldy closet offends my nose worse than a sewer.

In New York City we have many aged ladies who fill the elevator with pungent camphor smells when they exhume their ancient fur coats. Truly, I hate that smell.

Why camphor offends my nose I do not know—unless I was once a moth or even a butterfly. But I digress, and actors are not supposed to digress. We must stick to our lines. We are not writers.

When Belinda came home from the hospital we entered an impossible routine. She would lie in her bed seemingly lifeless for hours. We would make the decision to let her go and then she would perk up and drink water, eat a bite of food, and then lie lifeless again.

I would summon the vet to perform euthanasia. Then I would cancel the appointment. The decision was mine but I could not make it. Every time she got better, I would decide she was cured.

But Belinda had Addison's disease, so healing was a problem for her. The vets excised the lipoma on her hip, but the wound refused to heal. We tried everything from vacuum bandages to rare antibiotics that cost twenty dollars a capsule. We tried keeping her in a sterile chamber to isolate ourselves from the MRSA and E. coli she invariably developed. We spent a fortune on vets and veterinary hospitals.

"What shall we do, Belinda? Give me a sign, a bark, a bite, a lick. Talk to me."

I really felt she could talk but couldn't yet make up her

own mind. I seemed to have endless conversations with her in which we weighed the choices together, considered transmigration of souls, her last life, her next life, and mine. When would we ever meet again? On this planet or another? We were fated to be partners, that much I knew.

But her right hip had turned into a bloody cave with pus-covered muscles peeking through. What if I caught the MRSA or E. coli? What if my husband caught it? Or my pregnant daughter? I asked Belinda if she was ready to depart. She told me I had to make the decision—which was worse somehow than living in this limbo.

So I summoned the vet for the last time. I held Belinda's good paw while my vet injected her with forgetfulness. Her long pink tongue lolled out of her black lips. We closed her big brown eyes. And she was gone.

For months afterward I heard her skittering around the apartment. Sometimes a door would open and I'd be sure it was Belinda. Sometimes a gust of wind, a sigh, a soft, almost inaudible bark. I saw her on the floor at the foot of our bed. I saw her in the bathtub, where she preferred to sleep on hot summer nights. I saw her on the street being walked. I ached for her. But she was dead, and my mother, at almost a hundred, was still alive.

My near-centenarian progenitor had long since stopped being the fierce mother I had sharpened my teeth against. She now meandered between sleep and sentimentality. Speech eluded her—she who had once been so articulate.

Death can be—dare we say it?—a blessing. The Greeks—who knew everything—knew that immortality without youth was to be feared rather than desired. But who listens to the ancient Greeks? No one. Not even modern Greeks.

Watching my mother smiling in lipstick and pearls, I wondered about her insane tenacity and her low blood pressure.

"What if she outlives all of us?" I asked Isadora on the phone.

"She might," Isadora says. "But at least it won't be your problem."

I used to adore my mother. Then I used to despise her. I had spent my life bouncing between these poles like a demented magnet. I had imitated her, parodied her, pandered to her. I knew her death would not be an easy one for any of us. After all, I had spent many hours mourning my father—and what's a father compared to a mother? Not even a blood relative—as they say of husbands. Or, as Margaret Mead said: "A mother is a biological necessity, a father a social invention." Yet a father of daughters is a man who's been tested. And usually found wanting.

I can't write any of this. It's too damned mean. I used to have no problem being mean. But as I age, I censor myself. You can't be honest if you censor yourself. Mean is part of life and part of me. I have to let it rip. That's my job. Censorship is not my business.

It may be that we atheists are entirely wrong about heaven and hell. Suppose we die and discover that Dante was right in his description of the tortures of the damned? What will Chris Hitchens do then?

So, this is a story about heaven and hell. Just so you know. The hell of writing is self-censorship. The heaven is the freedom of speaking the truth. Women have a particular problem with this.

Not long ago, I reread Marguerite Yourcenar's *Memoirs of*

Hadrian. I was amazed to discover what she had written in her note about the difficult composition of the book—which had taken her many decades:

> Another thing virtually impossible, to take a feminine char-
> acter as a central figure . . . Women's lives are much too lim-
> ited or else too secret. If a woman does recount her own
> life she is promptly reproached for no longer being truly
> feminine.

We all struggle with this—still. The woman who chooses to write disguised as a male character is hoping to avoid the problem. But you cannot avoid the problem of being a woman.

A week after her birthday, I went to see my mother again. She was lying in bed not waking and not sleeping. Her skin looked much smoother. It was as if the wrinkles on her old face were disappearing, as if she were going back to being a baby. This frightened me. I saw it as a harbinger of her end and I panicked. I did not want to lose her.

I sat with her for an hour at least, trying to evoke some response from her. I rubbed her back, smoothed her hair, blathered about my day without any response.

"I love you so much," I said. "You were a great mother. I thank you for the acting, the rare books, the paintings, all the love you gave us. You were a wonderful mother and I love you."

No response. So I began again. "I love you so much and I thank you for everything. You were a great mother."

Again, no answer. Impossible to tell whether she heard me

or not. But my mother was sharp. I never could fool her. She knew when I was lying. She was my toughest critic. How could I judge what she knew or did not know? How could I judge her quality of life? Impossible. I thought death would release her, but maybe I was wrong. Maybe my valedictory tone upset her. Maybe she resented the past tense. Maybe I should speak in the present tense.

"I love you with all my heart," I said. "You are a wonderful mother."

"I love you more!" she exploded.

And that's my mother—fiercely competitive to the end, overwhelming us all with her longevity, refusing to die. She may have told the story of the baby eaglets and implied she was ready to be left in the nest alone—but it was not true at all. She wanted to hold us all captive. She would never let us go.

When we're born, we can't know if it will be into a nest of vipers or of sweet singing birds. And even the singing birds compete for worms flown in from mama bird, who is capricious with her worms and love. You think the love is equal until you are four or so and then another chick arrives and you are as awful to her as the older chick was to you, trying to peck out her eyes, sweetly singing all the time.

But we had to leave the nest and move on. The fact that my father died, that my mother sits atop her century like a black widow, holding us all eviscerated in her web, that my husband nearly died, does not give me a special dispensation nor excuse me from death. The fate of all humans is my fate. I am entitled to seize what's left of my life with joy.

11

More, More, More

Time can stand still, I am convinced of it; something
snags and stops, turning and turning, like a leaf on
a stream.

—John Banville, *The Untouchable*

Can you be joyful with a dead dog and a lingering centenarian mother? There's the rub. If only euthanasia were possible with mothers!

I am beginning to think that death may not be the worst thing that happens to a living creature. Lingering may be much worse.

I have always been a vivid dreamer. I can sleep for ten hours a night, dreaming endless dreams. After Belinda dies, the dreaming grows more intense.

I dream I am crossing a muddy river, my long skirt covered in slime. A dial is in my hand. How it got there I don't know, but it points to a number, 1888—and a young man with a dark, bushy handlebar mustache is crossing behind me, screaming at me in Russian. Terrified, as in a dream, I yell: "Not this far back!" I dial forward—1932—and there are my young parents swimming in the sea—without me.

"No!" I shout. "No!"

"Why do you think you can pick the time?" my mother asks me.

And forward goes the dial to some blurry number starting with 20 and four young people are staring into a coffin—and weeping. The corpse gets up—me—"Too late!" she says—"Too late."

I fiddle with the dial—which is made of light—and the numbers run in one direction, then another—like pages in a book you are trying to find a quote in. Can't find the right page, can't find the right page. There is a towheaded three-year-old on a beach, a teenager in a prom gown, a bride, another bride, then back again to my parents in Provincetown climbing a steep dune, then my grandfather escaping from Russia, then the coffin, then my parents again.

"No! No!" I want to wake up. But I can't wake up. I keep running back and forth in time, endlessly unable to find a fixed point. The dial spins. The light flickers—and here I am—but where I've stopped the clock I can't know.

Backward and I'm at the beginning of time. Forward—I'm dead. The dial keeps spinning as if it has a mind of its own. Which it does.

Imagine your life—the before and after of it. And imagine that projected against the curve of time. The dial of light races quickly forward and back. If you could see your life that way, where would you stop? And is it up to you? Can you decide which parallel universe to enter? Or is it all determined by a game of chance? Grandparents, parents, racing through time, throwing you out as if you were DNA dice, not knowing where you'll land.

Our deepest wish is to stop time, to slide between the branes of memory and outwit the Angel of Death. If I could stop time anywhere I would stop it when I met Asher and realized how right we were for each other. I remember our wedding, his love for my daughter, the hysterical laughter we still share. How can I dream of losing any of that? Clearly I am terrified by his illness.

Most of our lives don't last. The delusion of lasting is usually wrong. Fires and wars destroy papyrus, even animal skins. Paper rots. Digital files succumb to holocausts we can't yet imagine. The will to endure is strong, the fact of enduring usually wrong. Even our planetary tabula rasa won't last— though we go on as if it will. And here I am, trying to dial back age as if I were trying to hold back the ocean.

We think we have forever to fiddle with time, but we don't. Time is ruthless. It may be a "winged chariot," but it's a winged chariot bristling with automatic weapons. It's the ocean practicing oblivion. The wave is the meditative practice of the sea, say the Zen masters. But it means to wipe us out.

And now I am back staring at the lighted dial.

When I blast away from the tattered planet as if I were traveling by satellite, I can see the green earth turning brown in great dusty patches near the equator. Clods of earth turning to dust take off and fly into space. But my home city is drowned. Skyscrapers are up to their towers in seawater. Little boats, *motoscafi* from Venice, putter about trying to rescue old people before the towers crumble and fall. The old people—me!—don't want to depart with the rescuers. We used to imagine New York blasted by bombs when we were in elementary school. But soon New York may be flooded like Venice! Spin the dial backward if you can. Spin, spin, spin!

The thought of a flooded city reminds me of Venice when I was young and in love with a man who called me *pane caldo*—hot bread. We used to make love on his boat in the middle of the lagoon. Making love on a boat is like being on another planet. The waters of the planet engulfed and enfolded us as we rocked inside each other. Every motion of the boat brought him deeper inside me.

Young again, my whole body humming with the old energy, my heart in my mouth, my loping, skipping walk belonging to me again. And the horizon bobbing up and down, my feet spring up from the earth as if I could fly.

Everything has been so serious and now my riskiness is back. My life is a pogo stick, hopping.

I walk down the street no longer cursed with the invisibility of older women, followed by an invisible dog.

At least I am young again in my dreams. That will have to be enough. Perhaps my mother is also young again in *her* dreams and that is keeping her alive!

When you have been housebound with someone ill, you venture out onto the street as if for the first time. I knew New York intimately. And yet I didn't know it at all because New York is always in the process of being rebuilt. The city constantly shifts under our feet. It's like a primal planet with lava flows and storms and cacophonous noises. You always expect the ground to open under you and reveal the molten heart of the city. Perhaps that's why native New Yorkers are ready for anything—even our imminent destruction.

I wander east amid the troughs of what will never become the mythic Second Avenue subway, through the roaring traffic, and come upon an old man having an I-thou conversation with a hydrant.

"You're not just a water hole!" he shouts. And then something else—but I have known too many crazy people in my life to stick around. I admire an old woman with neon yellow hair piled on top of her head. And I pass another woman who has dyed her white dog the same fierce red color as her coiffure. Ah, the Upper East Side—home to the homeless, the crazies, the capillarily challenged.

Almost without planning it, I find my way to a church that has an AA meeting at noon-thirty. I have never gone to enough meetings, though I don't drink anymore. I've finally accepted that it depresses me. Downstairs, in the bowels of the earth, the lost souls are gathering. The chairs scrape on the floor. People cough and greet one another. The speaker commands the microphone.

She's an older woman I don't recognize. Her hair is white and wild and her makeup is perfect.

"I'm an alcoholic," she says, "and my name is Cynthia." She then begins a story of an alcoholic childhood—her parents alphabetized the booze in file cabinets—siblings who died of the disease, husbands who died of the disease, and several suicide attempts that didn't work.

"I can't believe I tried to shorten a life that is already so short. What was I thinking? I was furious at God. Now I know I was furious at myself. When we try to destroy ourselves, we are deluded. We believe we can escape from pain. But there is no escape. The only way to escape from pain is to join forces with your higher power. Get on your knees. Humble yourself. Ask for help. Unless you ask for help, help will never come. To be human is to be self-will run riot. The only way to happiness is surrender. Surrender is the key to everything. Surrender *is* everything. Surrender is peace. For most of my life I wanted More More More. Nothing was ever enough. I was full of envy and resentment. I thought everyone had more than I did. Now I know that the More More More obsession is a disease, a delusion. We all have enough. We just don't know it."

I shoot my hand up. "I have also suffered from the More More More disease," I say. "I am so grateful to you for mentioning it. I wanted more sex, more control, more money, more everything. More, More is a disease."

After the secretary's break, various people in the room compliment Cynthia on her wisdom, her kindness, her survival.

Why is it so hard to be a human being? I wonder. Why do we have to surrender? And to what? What if you refused to believe in a higher power? What if you thought *you* were the only trustworthy higher power? I have done that my whole life and I know it doesn't work. You are not enough. Your will is not enough. But God? God is a pagan dream, conjured out of neediness. God is a glitch in a too-big brain.

Glitch or not, we seem to need a power greater than ourselves. We seem to need enormous shadows of divinity stalking us. We know we are weak. Alcoholics are, above all, lonely, fearful people who make a fetish of loneliness, who think they—we—are too good to be part of the human race. And we have to be humbled to remember who we are—stumbling human beings, more ape than angel.

I have been through that with my daughter, with myself, with the men in my life. I need constant reminders of my vanity, my weakness, my foolishness. I am a human being who will die. What I do before that may matter or it may not. Only those who come after us will know.

Men have humbled me. Work has humbled me. Life has humbled me. I have to remember that ultimately I am just a bag of ashes like Belinda.

One member of the meeting says: "I loved your qualification. I also belong to the More More More Club."

More More More seems to have struck a chord because many people mention it. We are all so alike in our grievances, in our troubles.

After the meeting, the speaker comes up to me.

"Don't you remember me?" she asks.

I look at her blankly.

"We were in elementary school together on the Upper West Side."

I stare at her, looking for the little girl she was. I can't remember.

"You really reached people with what you said," she points out.

"Did I? I never know. But I always feel better when I speak."

"Amazing, isn't it?"

"We're all so similar. We all struggle over the same stuff. You'd think we'd know that by now."

"But we have to learn it again and again. I loved your

description of the liquor in file cabinets—V for vodka, R for rye, *S* for scotch," I say.

"When I was a kid, I thought everyone did that," Cynthia says.

Then other people come up to congratulate her and I bump straight into my friend Isadora Wing.

"I didn't even see you," I say.

"Well, I saw and heard you," she says. "Isn't it strange to find such intimate exchanges in the riot of New York. We descend into a church basement we never knew was there and total strangers are talking about the deepest things in their lives. Then they pack up and go away again. If we go often enough, we know many faces and names and the whole city will seem like a different place—like when you have a dog."

Fear is a universal emotion that nearly everyone struggles with, I think. But fear of what? Of pain? Of death? Of loss? It's pointless to fear death because death obliterates the fear of death. Loss of loved ones? You can't really prepare yourself for that no matter how hard you imagine it. It will always affect you differently than you thought it would. So fear is useless. It's just a way of blotting out the present and living in an imaginary future. Meetings have a way of dragging you back into the present. Why they work is impossible to tell. Why they bring a measure of peace is mysterious. We walk into the church basement in a tizzy and come out calm.

"I love you," Isadora says. "Gotta go."

Walking in New York. Isadora is right. When you feel fear, you have to lullaby it to sleep.

New York is full of all these secret worlds. The world of AA meetings. The world of theatrical people desperate for roles they'll never get or writers determined to finish books no one will read. Or violinists desperate because they haven't practiced enough. So much desperation. So much striving. The air is thick with it. You can feel it. And nothing in this world succeeds without sheer excess. Too much serenity doesn't do the trick. But that is the conundrum of New York or any striving place. You have to have moxie. You have to have guts. And then you have to know when to turn it off and surrender to the flow. Is everything about surrender?

The flow takes me smack into my former friend Nadya Nessim, who has just written a book about her amazing cunt. Nadya hasn't talked to me in several years, ostensibly because she didn't like the advice I gave her about her work. I should never have told her that she's making her readers feel bad. But there was more to it than that.

Nadya is a beautiful, redheaded narcissist, in love with her own reflection and unable to stand anyone who perceives any flaw in her beauty or her character. She's six feet tall and forever posing as if her profile is about to be photographed. Her first book was called *The Tragedy of Beauty*. I'd dared to question whether writing so self-adoringly might have distanced her readers. She did not take it well. She was a legend in her own mind and she hates any criticism.

"How are you, Ness?" Nadya asks, full of fake friendship. What's going on here? What does she want from me?

Female friendships are so strange. I had taken Nadya under my maternal wing when she was going through a dreadful divorce, had nurtured her, treated her like the daughter she wasn't until my own daughter got jealous and Nadya wanted More More More. They always want More More More. Glinda resented her deeply. Two beautiful redheads who hated each other.

Nadya is a creature of opportunistic ambition that she hides under a passion to change the world. Not to mention her own beauty. Mostly she wants to change the world to worship her uncritically, but she doesn't know this. She has less self-knowledge than nearly anyone I've ever met. It's sad. She's beautiful and smart but lacks emotional honesty.

"Not so great. My father died, my dog died, my husband isn't doing so well either."

"Can I buy you a drink?"

"I don't do that anymore. But you can have a drink and I can have something else."

"Great," says Nadya, and we duck into a dark bar-cum-brasserie on Second Avenue.

"I'm sorry I blasted you that time," Nadya says.

"Don't worry about it. I'm not holding a grudge."

"No, you were so generous to me, and I was completely ungrateful."

"Nothing to be grateful for. How's the new book?" I ask.

"Getting slammed by all my supposed sisters."

"That proves you must be doing something right."

"Do you really think so?"

"I'm sure of it," I say. " 'No one throws stones at a barren tree' goes the Arab proverb."

"But it hurts," says Nadya.

"I'm sure it does. I remember critics. One famous critic once called me 'a hyena in petticoats.' But just think—you remind people of how starved they are, and nobody likes that."

"But I'm trying to change that starvation," she says. "Where's the gratitude?"

"Gratitude is a word in the dictionary. If you're trying to

save the female sex to receive gratitude from them, forget it. Gratitude is the rarest of emotions. You must know that."

"But my book tries to teach them how to have sexual pleasure! I don't get it."

"I do," I say. "You're beautiful, famous, and have a handsome lover. That's enough. So many women are starving."

"Vanessa—you can't say that you accept the situation."

"I don't accept it, but I know that revolutionaries always end badly. Either they become dictators or they're killed off by their revolutionary colleagues. History shows us that. If you want to be a revolutionary, get used to the attacks. It's impossible to legislate sexuality."

"I can't believe you'd say that."

"Why?"

"Because you were always my inspiration. Long before I met you, I wanted to model my life on yours."

"Oy."

"Why oy?"

"Because I have never understood my life less. I've been through a very tough period."

"Tell me about it."

"I'd have to write a tome to tell you about it. And I don't write that sort of thing. Plays, screenplays. All they need is a good ear for dialogue."

"Well, I'm sure you could do it and maybe even change the world."

"I don't have much optimism about changing the world for the better. It's hard enough to change yourself for the better. I'm not sure that the word can save the world. The world is so fucked. And nobody listens to the word."

"You've really become a pessimist."

"Maybe I always was. The human race does not give me hope. We're despoiling the only planet we have, torturing and killing one another, treating women like shit in much of the world. This is insanity."

"But I think we can change things," Nadya says.

"By focusing on our pussies? I've always been for pussy—yes. But you'd be surprised how few women have the leisure to focus on their pussies—not to mention no partners. That's why you piss them off."

"But I *want* them to have partners."

"So do I, but it's more complicated than wishing. You tell them about how great their sexual potential is, how wonderful their cunts are—all of which is true—and they go home with their vibrators or their bumbling boyfriends. Naturally, they resent you. It's really sad. They would love to have the orgasms you describe, the orgasms you can have—but they're starving. It's like the starving child with nose pressed against the window of a fabulous pastry shop. How can you tempt the starving with satiety?"

"Of course I know that, Vanessa, but I want to change it."

"Then get them all fabulous tantric lovers who can awaken them."

"I wish I could," I say.

"It *is* a problem—once you know your potential, you long for its fulfillment."

I flash on my own stunted sex life. I know what I'm capable of and I know Nadya has described it—but how hard it is to find, especially with an old husband. An old, sick husband. There it is. I said it.

"I know," Nadya says. "You worry me." But Nadya can't know yet. Nadya doesn't know the half of it. Nobody knows until they get to that point—an ailing husband, the lack of zipless fucks, or even zipped-up fucks. Not to mention the fantasy of the "happily married woman" with sex on the side.

How can you have tantric sex "on the side"? When sex is that great, it takes up your whole life, your imagination, your dreaming. You would fly anywhere for it, sail your boat across the Mediterranean, ask your deck monkeys to tie you to the mast before you dove into it again. It's the life force, the fire that goes from loins to navel, navel to heart, heart to brain. It's everything—particularly creativity. And I miss it. I miss it all the more because I can remember having had it.

"I worry myself lately," I say.

As I walked home from my meeting with Nadya, I thought about all the people who'd tried to change the lot of women through the centuries and how often things had gone back to the way they were. Were women their own worst enemies? Did we allow ourselves to be envious of other women to the detriment of our own progress? Or was it just that young females were so *fartutst* about getting their waiting eggs fertilized that they forgot about liberty? You could never forget about it. You had to keep on fighting forever.

I think Aldous Huxley was right about reproduction in *Brave New World*. Until we could "decant" sperm and egg separate from partners, we'd never have equality. Men were too territorial and violent. But detach reproduction from human relationships and you might have a chance.

We all ought to be *hatched*. Then we could choose our own preferred parents rather than being stuck with the ones we were born from. We'd create "chosen families." Would I have chosen my particular mother? I doubt it. But I probably would have chosen my father—ah, my poor dead daddy. I missed him so. I was number one on his hit parade and my sisters never let me forget it.

Envy was what corrupted the world of women. Of course, men were envious too, but they knew they had to kill one another until they figured out a viable pecking order. Then they fell into their appointed—or anointed—places—at least until the alpha male began to fail. We women didn't really know how to do that. We pretended not to believe in hierarchies, to all be sisters under the skin—till hell broke loose. It was a very defective system for stability. Better to be hatched into a particular caste and stay there. Yes, I was becoming horribly pessimistic. Who was it who said, "Whoever is not a misanthrope by forty can never have loved mankind?" That was me—despondent, deranged, depressed.

Of all the ills we are heir to, depression is the worst. Looking down at your slippers in the morning and not believing it's worthwhile to put them on is like waking in a dungeon of doom. Not bothering to shower and dress because you've seen it all, known it all, and don't care anymore is a torture beyond nightmares. I have been to that dark place. I never want to be trapped there again. It used to be sex that got me out—sex and falling in love. What can get me out now? Zipless.com? I wish. I could hardly think about Zipless without being grateful for Asher in my life. Thank the Goddess he had never found out.

———

On the way home, I stopped into a high-end deli where the food could have been weighed out in solid gold. It was three in the afternoon and at the sparsely occupied tables were mostly ancient women—almost as old as my mother. They were all speaking different languages—Russian, Polish, Portuguese. And eating with a gusto that was almost biblical. The joy of food remains to the very old—if nothing else. And all these women looked like witches—jawbones and noses prominent, eyes sunken in orbits of bone, backs crooked and shoulders moving upward as they shoveled in the food. Often they were wearing battered hats that had gone out of fashion wars ago.

This was where we all were going—Botox or no tox, lifts or not. We would all be witches someday—maybe that was what my play was about? Most of us would be alone, some with old girl friends with whom we shared a language if not complete trust. We were all going down that twisting path that led you-know-where. We'd break our staffs and burn our books once we'd seen our daughters married off and becoming mothers. We were all Sycorax or Prospera or even Gaia. What did we have to fear? Everything. Nothing. Nothingness.

My telephone gave a little ping. There were some pages that described a flight through outer space. At first, I thought this might be a message from one of the swains—but no, these seemed to be pages from Isadora:

> We journeyed through the vastness of the stars. In the black sky we saw bright lights—some blue, some yellow, some golden. We got used to this journey and after several months stopped asking, "Are we there yet?" The odyssey lasted weeks, years, eons. Children were born. Grandparents

died. More children were born. We didn't ask if the children were boys or girls. It seemed irrelevant. All we cared about was the endless voyage. It was as if we had all turned into Odysseus and we were fated to travel forever while the gods above us took bets on our futures.

Athena was there and Aphrodite. Zeus was playing dice with the universe. Hermes, the messenger of the gods, flew with his winged sandals from galaxy to galaxy, bringing messages from gods to people. Time seemed to disappear. Time, anyway, is an illusion, as is death. Eventually, we landed on an asteroid. On shaky sea legs we climbed out of our ship.

What was this planet? Rusty red with huge blue stones veined with gold. The atmosphere was so rich in oxygen that we could not walk but ran. We bounced. We felt like characters out of some myth, treading on air.

Very hard to evoke something so unfamiliar, but we were elated by our new home. The air must also have been full of some substance that made us all laugh and sing simultaneously. We sang, we sang, we sang. If you can sing, you know your problems are not insurmountable.

What was Isadora writing about? A new world in which the troubles of humanity were extinguished? I read on and on and on, thinking, My old friend has flown into space! And then I shut my phone down and ordered food.

I bought a thick slice of duck pâté and a spinach salad for Asher, knowing he would love it. It gave me pleasure to have him waiting at home, knowing it might not always be the case. Feeding men and children was very satisfying, especially when we knew that someday we'd only have to feed ourselves. All the chores we'd once complained about became life-affirming now. Life-affirming. Life-enhancing. Life.

My phone pinged urgently. The man with the rubber sex suit would not give up, would not give up, would not give up. My lack of response excited him.

"R U REALLY HAPPILY MARRIED?" he demanded.

"YES," I texted back. On some level, I knew it was true.

Dear Goddess, how did my generation get feminism so wrong? Yes, we needed to change both custom and law. Yes, we needed Betty and Gloria and Germaine and Andrea and Shulamith and Alix and Erica and Nora and the girl guides at Berkeley who rescued Emma Goldman from undeserved obscurity. What a great woman she was to know that a real revolution also included dancing! And did she ever give up sex with men? Never!

How much the ideologues got wrong. How were we ever going to exclude our fathers and grandfathers and brothers and sons and husbands—all of them—and mentors and pals? We didn't spring full grown from the egg of time. We had mentors and lovers and partners and pals who believed in us. Even I, stumbling behind the great girl guides in my dirty tennis shoes, had men who were loving mentors. Lep loved my acting, my writing, my wit. And my father and grandfather adored me, tried to teach me all they knew of life and love and lucre. I realized that the true secret of my confidence was being loved by my father and grandfather.

Was it their fault that it took me so long to grow up? Hardly. I was given the seeds of the pomegranate on a golden plate and refused to eat, thinking I knew better.

And now, when I am surrounded by death—yet still, somehow, dancing—I know that I was born to give life as well as art and that both are equally important.

If I were offered it now, I would eat the pomegranate and stash the golden plate in a safe-deposit box for my daughter to melt down when she was ready!

PART III

Spring

12

Grandmothering

This is My covenant, which ye shall keep, between Me and you and thy seed after thee: every male among you shall be circumcised. And ye shall be circumcised in the flesh of your foreskin; and it shall be a token of a covenant betwixt Me and you. And he that is eight days old shall be circumcised among you, every male throughout your generations, he that is born in the house, or bought with money of any foreigner, that is not of thy seed. He that is born in thy house, and he that is bought with thy money, must needs be circumcised; and My covenant shall be in your flesh for an everlasting covenant. And the uncircumcised male who is not circumcised in the flesh of his foreskin, that soul shall be cut off from his people; he hath broken My covenant.

—Genesis 17: 10–14

My cell phone shrieked. It was Glinda.

"Mom—I'm in labor," my daughter said. "Meet me at the hospital."

So once again I took off for that place where so many life passages begin and end. This time it was Mount Sinai, where the maternity ward is full of orthodox Jews in old-fashioned hats and new-fashioned wigs.

On the way, I called Isadora.

"You are a most unconvincing grandma," she said. "You look too damned young."

Glinda was in a labor room breathing with her husband, Sam, who looked pale and terrified. I thought of tribes who had the husbands wade out into the sea with the menfolk while their wives were in labor. It seemed like a better plan than our own isolated hospital waiting. What can a man do for his wife at a time like this? My then-husband, Glinda's father, Ralph, aka Rumi, shot videos when I was in labor that seemed more obscene at the time than pornography. For God's sake, do something useful—like not drowning. Husbands are not meant to be doulas. It gets them upset.

I liked being pregnant, but I would have happily skipped the whole birthing process. If I could have been knocked out cold like a 1930s mom, I wouldn't have minded. But in my day, there was endless propaganda about "natural childbirth." There is, in my view, nothing natural about childbirth—but death. Before modern medicine, mothers and babies died like flies—as they still do in much of the world. The one thing childbirth taught me was not to romanticize nature. Red in tooth and claw, tending toward annihilation of the most vulnerable, nature is not all that great. I nearly died trying to deliver Glinda "naturally"—a delusory effort on my part. I labored for nine hours (it seemed like ninety) before giving up and having a C-section—possibly considered defeatism by my feminist cohort. But thank the Goddess for C-sections.

Sadly, Glinda was doomed to repeat this pattern—since we both have cervixes that don't dilate readily. But at least she had the C-section sooner. Not soon enough for her over-identified mother.

But when the baby appeared, wrapped in his pink-and-blue striped cap, swaddled in receiving blankets, shut-eyed, red-faced, and wrinkly, we found him the most gorgeous creature we'd ever beheld. He weighed nearly nine pounds, aced all his neonatal tests, and clearly was a genius. Glinda and Sam called him Leonardo after da Vinci. And we called him Leo.

He reduced us to simpering idiots, finding family resemblances in this new creature who looked like every other baby. We saw in him the future—a thing we'd not believed in for a long time. We marveled over his perfect hands and feet, his

lusty cry, his endearing little kicks. This was a perfect creature that we all had made.

A baby! Then the human race will continue despite all our
moronic mistakes—not to mention those of our political lead-
ers. What is it about babies? We are hardwired to adore their
little feet and hands, their oceanic eyes, their coos, their
gurgles, their vomit, their pee, their sweet-smelling baby poop.
At least I was. Leo reduced me to my primal maternal essence. I was the ur-matriarch, ready to give my all to this
incredible nine pounds of hope.

As for Glinda, she delighted in telling and retelling the
story of her giving birth—embellishing with each retelling.
Her labor got longer and longer, her bleeding more and more
excessive, her heroism greater.

I am not knocking this. The heroism of mothers makes
the world go round. We cannot give it enough credit. And
we don't.

A friend once told me that before you visit your grandchildren, you get more excited than when you are going to meet a
lover. Mostly it's true. Your focus shifts in a crucial way. All
your lovers pale before this little squirming lump of hope. The
future! And you are already a part of it—through no fault of
your own!

Also the dead children on TV become real to you in an
excruciating way—children killed by drones, land mines,
earthquakes, kidnappers become your own children. You used
to be a smokin' broad but now you are a smokin' grandma
and all the world's children are your own children. If only
we could organize all the grandmas of the world—that
might really work. Grandmas may be the only women in the
world to understand the proper place of men. We ought to

unite to change the world! Grandmotherhood had brought back hope.

Holding Leo, inhaling his aphrodisiacal newborn scent, I was transported to Babyland—a land of harmony where sleep comes easily, milk flows like tears, and all is well. "How many miles to Babyland?" went an old song playing in my memory. Where did it come from? It was lost in the amnesia of early childhood. If only I could retrace these snatches of memory.

What came back to me was Glinda's infancy—how I stared and stared at her, finding perfection in every finger, every toe, how I loved nursing her, listening to the gurgling of her stomach, her pooping as I switched her from one breast to the other; my complete delight in what a friend of mine called "the tube stage of life." In one hole and out the other—how simple and elemental! It was so much more satisfying than an audition or waiting for reviews. You got your review then and there—and it was good.

But Glinda hated breast-feeding—perhaps because there was so much propaganda for it.

My sister Antonia made it all worse by coming in and declaring, "Just pretend you're a monkey."

"But I'm not a monkey," Glinda said. "Do people really *like* this?"

I knew that if I said I liked it, she'd be even more determined *not* to breast-feed. So I said nothing. Saying nothing is the deep wisdom of grandmothering. Shut up, Grandma, your kids cannot possibly accept that you know *anything*!

I had adored breast-feeding for six months or so—that elemental stage of existence, the feeding and excretion that consumes the lives of most living creatures. And I had wept when the baby began to wean herself because she was a big baby and started getting more substantial food. Besides, after six months or so, you start feeling trapped by the baby's schedule, and milk pumping had to be done by hand with little plastic trumpets in my day. Still, I would not have missed breast-feeding for the world. It was such a simple way of being needed and fulfilling a loved one's need. It was sensual to me, exciting and fulfilling both.

New ecological mothering was all the rage with Glinda's generation. You were supposed to sleep with your baby, transport your baby in a sling, use cloth diapers, and food-process your own baby food. Motherhood had been turned into a time-and-a-half job in rebellion against my feminist generation. Young women felt madly superior to their mothers because of all that slinging, food-processing, co-sleeping, and rigid observance of Dr. and Nurse Sears's method of baby farming. Parenting—already a twenty-four-hour-a-day job— now became a thirty-six-hour-a-day job, and mothers were fiercely proud of it.

I had always believed in baby nurses despite the fact that they were mostly difficult control freaks, so I paid for a baby nurse. She was called Drusilla. She was a bossy Belizean who knew everything and wouldn't let you forget it.

Baby nurses hate mothers who nurse. That took care of Glinda's reluctance to do it. Gone was the breast pump, and for Glinda it was good riddance.

I was not about to go on about how I'd enjoyed it. I believe that each mother should find her own way of mothering, that all the advice we give on mothering is useless. It's hard enough to be a mother without having some book or blog to obey. But the blogging that went on about breast-feeding and new mothering! Women are so competitive about their tits! You'd think we'd just invented them.

I know how illuminating it is to suddenly discover the wisdom of the body when you've spent much of your life denying the body and its vast intelligence.

But the breast-feeding part was easy compared to what came eight days later—the bris. The bris, the Brit Milah, the covenant of circumcision. Or as I like to think of it: Next time, boychick, we take the whole thing! Who would have believed I'd be wandering around my apartment looking for anesthetizing cream to put on his cute little dick while my daughter forbade me to get near her son!

As you've already gathered, the bris was at my house. Asher was thrilled to host it. All our friends and Glinda's and Sam's, waiting to behold the ancient sacrificial rite. My darling shrink tells me I'm wrong about all this—but what the hell. She believes in circumcision—so do many wise people.

The mohel was from Jewish Central Casting. He had a sonorous rabbi voice, masses of curly dark hair, and sad eyes that told the story of the wandering Jew, and he told jokes endlessly. He reminded me of an old joke about mohels.

What did the mohel put in his window?

A bonsai tree.

Why a bonsai tree?

What else should a mohel put in his window?

The circumcision of my first grandson was a revelation to me.

Ever wonder why Jewish boys are so fucked up about sex?

Ever wonder why they fall for mile-high models from Slovenia who wear those big gold crosses? Ever wonder why Jewish boys fall in love with Chinese girls or blond shiksa cheerleaders from Kansas or those cool black models who dance like Beyoncé?

It's clearly because of the covenant with Yahweh or God. *I take this piece of your pecker, with your mother, father, grandfathers, and grandmothers looking on, exultant. And you think of nothing but your pecker for the rest of your life!*

Of course most men think of nothing but their pricks for most of their lives. But Jewish men do it better—or worse, depending on your point of view.

You think female circumcision is bad? (It's hideous, health-destroying and horrible—and inflicted on women by other women.) But at least women have other things to think about than their pussies—like children, like politics, like acting. At least women don't focus nonstop on their vaginas (or as Oprah says, their vajayjays). Men think about their pricks for the rest of their lives. Don't get me wrong, they think about them whether or not they're circumcised. But circumcision bumps it up to a whole other level.

Health reasons, my ass. It's the health of the old impotent grandpas they're thinking of, not you, little boy. You could learn to push the skin back and wash. We're not in the desert anymore. We have Jacuzzis and steam showers and redwood hot tubs from California—or Californicate, as I always called it, even before the TV show.

No, folks, it's the *grandpas* who love this ritual. The mothers usually run in the other room crying. But they get blamed for it anyway. And Jewish women bear the brunt ever after. Either the nice Jewish boys marry you and run around with

Diana Ross or Beyoncé or Naomi Campbell—or they marry
Sandra Oh or Lisa Ling or Yoko Ono and the converts.

In the old days, your mother used to threaten suicide. Now
we're more liberal, so your mother embraces Ms. Hung,
Ms. Jong, Ms. Ono, Ms. Liu, Ms. Hoe, Ms. Loe, Ms. Cho,
Ms. Choi, Ms. Loi. And guess what, the next little boy goes
through it anyway!

In my parents' youth, there was a show that ran forever in
which a Jewish boy fell head over heels in love with an Irish
lass. It was called *Abie's Irish Rose*. That was the forbidden
fruit in 1920s, 1930s New York. If you updated it, you'd have
to call it *Abie's Chinese Lotus* or *Tantric Tootsie*. The idea would
be the same: brilliant Jewish boy flees his mother and high-
tails it for India or China or Japan. (And you can find India,
Africa, and China right here in New York City. You don't even
have to take a plane.) Now everyone intermarries routinely.
Great for the gene pool if not for Jewish mothers.

Okay. Call me an anti-Semite. (I'm secretly a pro-Semite.)
But I do have misgivings about circumcision. And I have met
(and married) a lot of Jewish men. The *alter kockers* (delicately
translated as "old farts") have every explanation under the sun.
Explanations, after all, are all *alter kockers* can do. Circumcision is healthy, they claim. It prevents the clap. You won't get
those nasty new viruses that are around today, God forbid.
(A secret warning about gayness, I think.) But how can you
ever forget the pain, the fear, the confusion of being eight
days old and having your pecker snipped?

"They don't remember," say the *alter kockers*—who also
don't remember that *alter kocker* really means "old shitter."

"They don't feel it," say the *bubbes*.

"We did it in the hospital," say the parents.

"He didn't feel a thing," says the mother (who was in the other room crying her eyes out).

And here comes the mohel, with his beard, his tallis, his yarmulke, with his red wine and his gauze pads, his shiny snipper and his old jokes. Some of them actually suck off the snipped foreskin of the infant child and call it orthodoxy. (But every organized religion does absurd stuff—give me disorganized spirituality any day. At least then you can *choose* your own silly rituals.)

If this is the covenant with God, then God is a sadist. But we knew that already. He descends from Baal and all those other mean old gods. Not that the goddesses are any better. Think of Kali, after all, with her necklace of skulls. Life and death are always close as twins.

Even Jesus was circumcised, and many claim that Jesus was chaste—having demoted Mary Magdalene from disciple to whore, from wife to mistress, from wise woman to bimbo. But I never believed that version of the story. Now we supposedly have written proof that Jesus was possibly married—and probably to the woman most like his mother, that other Mary.

In the older Christianity—the one Jesus the Jew actually practiced—women were revered for their wisdom and spirituality. But that didn't suit Saint Paul, nor the apocalyptic Saint John (who was doubtless doing LSD on Patmos, where I visited his cave). When he wrote about the four horsemen and the blazing fires in the sky, he might well have been. Those horsemen might have been the Patmos sunset seen by a stoner emerging from a cave—or the Patmos sunrise—equally bewitching.

But whatever the old guys say, circumcision must hurt—even to a baby eight days old who then gets his first taste of wine—pain and alcoholism going hand in rubber glove.

It killed me to see my grandson marked like this so future Nazis could identify him. What is *wrong* with my chosen people? Are we chosen for *pain*? All the psychological troubles of Jewish men—from Sigmund Freud to Lenny Bernstein to Philip Roth—must stem from this dubious ritual. I want to tell my adorable grandson, *Just make sure you never make pee-pee in front of a skinhead*. But at eight days old, he doesn't know what a skinhead is!

Don't stigmatize him! Don't let guys in the men's room know he's Jewish! I wanted to shout, but instead I laughed hysterically at all the mohel's jokes.

"What a great audience!" he said, thinking my mad laughter was applause rather than anxiety. And then he was off to the next snip.

I'm no scholar of Judaism, but may I remind my chosen people that the bris begins with Abraham, who was willing, if not quite pleased, to sacrifice Isaac until God stopped him and substituted a spring lamb—or was it a goat? This always makes me think that the bris was a stand-in for human sacrifice. Those ancient religions were pretty bloody affairs.

Just sayin'.

But foreskin or no foreskin, I adored that perfect little Jewish boychick. Who wouldn't?

13

Wormhole

Everything, even herself, was now unbearable to her.
She wished that, taking wing like a bird, she could
fly somewhere, far away to regions of purity, and
there grow young again.

——Gustave Flaubert, *Madame Bovary*

Again I have that strange dream where I am going backward and forward in time. But this time I wake up in hideous pain. I am in the abortionist's office on Fifty-seventh Street.

"I don't belong here—I'm a grandmother now," I tell the nurse.

"You'll be fine," she says. "You're just a little disoriented."

"No, I am not—what year is it? I don't belong here!"

"Shhh," she says. "I can give you something for the pain."

And she goes to get me pills and water.

My head is scrambled. I wanted to go back in time to be young again—but not to feel this way. Besides, I no longer want to go back in time. Now that I'm a grandmother, I want to stay where I am!

The pills are white. The water is lukewarm. The nurse is not really listening to me.

"You'll be fine," she says, giving me the pills.

"I don't mean the pain, I mean I'm in the wrong time!"

"Breathe deeply," she says calmly. "The D and C went fine." And she gives me a shot that puts me to sleep.

I dream that I am Leo's grandmother at his bris. I dream Glinda's pregnancy and labor. But when I wake up, it is still the New York of my teenage years—old Fifty-seventh Street, near the old Russian Tea Room. The window I see is dark with soot and the sky is darkening. I stumble up and gaze out the sooty window at the Steinway store, the thrift shop where they sell old furs, the shabby delis. How do I get out of here? Why did I ever wish to be young again?

I think of all the time-travel movies I've seen and the books about time travel I've read. Everyone talks about getting to the past or the future—nobody tells you how to get back! You think you'll go back to the great things about youth—the energy, the unlined face, the rampant sexuality. But what if you go back to the *worst* things about your youth—like this? "Why do you think you can choose!" comes my mother's voice, chiding me. "You always think you can choose! *Some choices are permanent, Vanessa!*"

I look carefully again, searching for a Starbucks or some shop from today, but I can't find one. And everyone is wearing hats! I must be in the past since this is a world of hats. I want to go back to sleep and wake up at Glinda's apartment, staring at my grandson, Leo. I don't want to relive my horrible adolescence!

And then I see it—down the block from the Steinway store is Bibliomania, which in the fifties and sixties was in an old, now-demolished building, on the north side of Fifty-seventh Street. I begin to weep uncontrollably.

The doctor runs in with a bottle of whiskey and a cut-crystal highball glass (remember those?).

"What's wrong? Is it the bleeding? It's completely normal to bleed and cramp a bit, and some women feel sad. Don't worry, you'll feel much better soon. This will help." And he poured me a tumbler full of warm scotch.

"I'm sober," I say between sobs.

"You're *what?*"

"In the program. I don't drink."

"What program?"

Oh God, I must really be back in time, because nobody knew what "the program" was back then. I start to howl hideously. And loudly.

The doctor, of course, is terrified by all the noise I'm making. He's done something highly illegal and now he must think he's done it to a crazy girl who will report him.

"Lie down and rest," he says sternly.

In a little while, the nurse comes in and gives me another shot. I am sure this is it—the end of my life. I've read about abortion doctors who risked their patients' lives so as not to get caught. As my consciousness fades, I focus on Leo's sleeping baby face.

"What were you dreaming?" Asher asks, "You were talking in your sleep. Are you okay?"

I look at Asher's face with immense relief. Since his aneurysm, Asher has become a different man: mellow, empathic, full of the joy of being alive. Some men achieve this if they live long enough. They become wise.

"Bless you!" I say. "I was back in my adolescence. I thought it was real."

"Dreams can give you information," Asher says, "if you read them right. Dispatches from the dark side."

Mind still sozzled with sleep, I hug him.

"Nessy," he murmurs, a name from our galloping courtship, which I haven't heard for a long time.

I am half in and half out of the past when he kisses me slowly and tenderly on my mouth.

"Let me brush my teeth," I mutter.

"Forget it." And he slips down to caress my pussy.

"I have to pee," I say.

And I run to the bathroom, glad for the present, happy to have left the past behind, happy to be the age I am.

"Come back!" Asher calls urgently.

"Coming!"

I slip into bed, amazed that Asher is making the first move—which is unusual for him.

While I lie next to him, astounded by his presence still, he opens my silk robe and touches my cunt as if he were Adam just discovering Eve's pussy.

"Beautiful," he says.

And then he begins to run his tongue slowly along my labia, gently inserting one finger to feel for my G-spot on the front wall of wet pussy.

For one second, I remember the cramping and pain of the abortion's office, then I remind myself to *feel*, not think, to allow the warmth, the pleasure to flood over me, to unlock myself to his tongue, to surrender completely.

When you meditate, disruptive thoughts float in and out but you make a decision to let them go. So with pleasure. You decide to let go of the interruptions, the thinking, the distraction, the chastising voices of the past.

His tongue on my clit is lazy at first, then less lazy, then insistent as he touches my G-spot with his finger and I am swept away with waves of anticipation that blank out my mind and let me focus only on pleasure, releasing the painful past, releasing the desire to return there and be young and beautiful again. *Fuck* young and beautiful—this is worth everything—and I come with fierce contractions that seem to go on and on endlessly.

Asher holds me.

"I felt a bolt of lightning go down my spine when you came," Asher mumbles. "Incredible. Never felt anything like it before."

"You raised the kundalini," I say.

"What the fuck is that?"

"What you felt—like an electric snake in your spine."

"If you say so. It was amazing."

"It was."

"The kundalini is life force, energy, fire, sexual power. Some yogis believe that when you harness that body power to the mind, there's nothing you can't do. When you have that fire—sexuality, creativity, knowledge—everything comes together."

"You betcha. Kundalini, schmundalini—it's great stuff. I thought I was dying. You've brought me back."

"I think you may have done the same for me."

I remembered that when I first met Asher, he seemed to be at war with his body. We'd go to some amazingly beautiful spot in the world, stay in a gorgeous hotel suite where I immediately thought of sex, and he began by fussing with his various communication devices—CrackBerries, satellite phones, computers—keeping me away with his obsessive need to check in with his office. It made me crazy. I'd strip down to my silk underwear and dance around the suite, trying to attract him, and he would get pissed off at me. He felt controlled by my sexuality, thought I was using him as a relaxation device (and why not?) and would become ever more intent on resisting me. He made me utterly crazy and from time to time I would take off and meet an old lover just out of horniness and the feeling of rejection. Once I met a former lover of mine in the Crillon in Paris in one of those rooftop dormer suites for two days of amazing sex. There is a picture of me taken by a paparazzo who nearly, but didn't, out me, and I look more beautiful and glowing than I ever have in a tabloid picture. The reason was forty-eight hours with Franco, my old lover from Florence. Sex can do that—make your skin rosy and your eyes full of light—and nobody has to know but you and your lover. I felt I deserved to feel and look that good. No guilt at all. When you have taken off your clothes enough in the theater, no costume change seems to matter. Maybe that's why actors are so promiscuous. It feels like another part you're playing—as such part of work not play. But since your work *is* play, guilt is superfluous.

Was that why I was able to time-travel back to my past? Nothing really explained it—except my fierce wish to be young again, now gone. I was so relieved at being home, with Asher, that I wanted to atone for all my dangerous wishes to juggle time. I was terrified, in fact, that I might fall through wormholes without wanting to.

Wormholes were wishes, weren't they? And they were always there, waiting to suck you through. You never knew when the most painful part of your past might swallow you—just as you dreamed of returning to the best of your past—whatever that was. The point was that time was not in your control. Why did you believe it was? How arrogant!

I began to read everything I could find about time travel—Einsteinian relativity warps, parallel universes, the history of time-travel literature. It was a subject that never ceased to fascinate people—like raising the kundalini through sex. But the more I read about it, the less I could understand my own experience of it. Was it just that I'd always been a very vivid dreamer? Or had I somehow broken time's bonds through the power of wishing? I knew how powerful wishes could be. Whenever I wished hard enough for something, I got it. I had to be careful what I wished for then or I might outfox myself. But I was closing in on the end of the play despite my fears. I discovered the secret of writing—live in the present moment. Do not fantasize about possible response because you cannot know the future.

I knew that time travel was partly fueled by wishes. When I began my play about growing young again, I had interviewed many witches and studied many grimoires, and I knew that witchcraft without wishes—that is to say *intention*—probably would not work. *You needed intention above all.*

Meanwhile, Asher and I were growing closer and closer. His near-death experience had opened him up somehow. And I was opened up too. I was reminded of how overwhelming real passion could be, how it could become your raison d'être, and how few people wanted to acknowledge that. The poets did and the songwriters did. But most people wanted to forget it when it was no longer in their lives. Too disturbing. Too frightening. You missed it too much if you remembered well. Some men and women searched for it endlessly in one-night stands. But women didn't always love zipless fucks without a sense of safety and caring. Men often found pure lust disappointing—it depended on the man and where he was in his life. Real tantric sex was a *sometime* joy, as the ancients knew. It had to be much more than what my late friend Anthony Burgess called "the old in-out." It needed time, stroking, intention, eye contact, bathing together. It was inefficient—and that was part of the pleasure of it. American sexuality was too much like American work—goal oriented. The goal was the mutual orgasm. But tantric sex didn't covet *only* the goal, and that made it alien to a lot of Americans. Not that orgasm was unimportant, but it wasn't all there was. The whole body was the instrument of the sexual symphony, and most people missed it. I missed it too at this point in my life.

But I was glad that Asher and I were growing closer. That was a happy change. If only I could stay in the present and not be drawn back to the past.

Was my need for passion drawing me back into the past? In my past I'd known many varieties of passion—including some that were terrifying and devouring, some in which I thought I was being eaten alive by my need for a certain lover. I wanted to feel that again and never to feel that again. Could you feel that again at any age? Was it even possible?

My cell phone still accompanied me everywhere like an electronic genie. But I was less and less interested in its pagan pings.

If some man who could spell, who was beyond rubber suits and impersonating long-dead poets contacted me, then maybe, maybe I would get interested, but until then, my experiment with ziplessness had lost its savor. I wanted the growing closeness with my husband more than I wanted strangers. Astonishing.

14

A Language Beyond Language

I imagine that yes is the only living thing
——E. E. Cummings

It takes a long time to be born and a long time to die," my sister says, walking into our mother's room.

But this time it seems like the time might be here. She is staring vacantly into space, drooling, and seems utterly unaware we are here. Her caregiver, Ariella, is spooning diluted cereal into her mouth. She eats and drinks less and less.

The palliative care team has sent a secret box we are not supposed to open till they arrive and a decongestant that makes her very sleepy.

She has an oxygen tank by her bedside, which Ariella, a beautiful Haitian with high cheekbones, uses intermittently. She has given her, at doctor's orders, minute doses of morphine by mouth to ease her pain.

Despite all this, Ariella says, "She's fighter. She could wake up at any moment."

This time, I haven't wanted to tell my friends anything because she might well come to life again. And when I walk into her room, saying, "I'm here, I love you," she turns her head and starts babbling nonsense syllables—trying to talk, but this time it's a full gurgle, spewing saliva.

She used to go *ay yi yi yi*. Now she sees my red-and-purple shirt and tries to react to the color with sound. My mother has totally given up control.

How do I know this when she can't speak? I know it because I know her and her love for bright colors. I must have worn this especially for her. Of course I did.

But Ariella lifts her in her electric bed and she gurgles madly, trying to smile at my shirt.

"You always loved red and purple!" I say. And the gurgles increase.

"She's answering you," Ariella says, and I know this is true, but she is exhausted and sinks back down.

"This is my last job like this," Ariella says. "It's too hard. All these years with your mother and watch her go down. It's too hard. But I am glad to know her. She was like my mother." And Ariella begins to cry.

We think we know how death comes, having seen it before, but every death is as unique as every birth. There is no template that applies to everyone.

In the past I used to spend hours with my mother listening to her babbling nonsense. It was not easy. Now I began to understand that it was also a communication. "There is a language beyond language," Rumi, the great Sufi sage, says.

"She's going downhill," her Polish caregiver, Karolina, used to say.

"Every day she sleeps more. I tell you and your sisters the truth, the whole truth, and nothing but the truth. She's going downhill—like on a one-horse sleigh."

I used to have long philosophical conversations with

Karolina because I could no longer speak to my mother. Karolina had become her speaking voice. My mother wouldn't like the Polish accent but I know she'd like to have a *voice*. She was glad to use Karolina's voice—or now Ariella's.

"Ayyy yi yi yi" is pretty much all she could say then, and we had no idea why she said it. "Ayy yi yi yi yi," she'd repeat.

"Why ayy yi yi?" Karolina would ask.

"Why ay yi yi?" I'd answer, knowing nothing.

I had never heard those sounds from her in the past.

And my mother could not answer. She, the queen of Scrabble games with the seven-letter words, she of the brilliant IQ, she of the famous Gertrude, the brilliantly reviewed Mother Courage, and the great Lady Macbeth. She of the portraits in oil, in watercolor, in conté crayon. She of the rare first editions. Now she has been reduced to *ayy yi yi*.

"Ayy yi yi," I echo. "Ayy yi yi."

For most of my childhood, I believed my mother was right about everything. I echoed her tastes in theater, in art, in music, in books, in politics. Until the dread age of thirteen, I followed her lead in everything. And then I began to rebel— *ayy yi yi*.

"Mother, I love you," I'd say to the *ay yi yi*s.

Did a small curl in her wrinkled lip indicate the beginning of a smile? I couldn't tell. Within a minute or two she would seem to be sleeping again.

And now she sleeps, even more deeply. Is death like dreamless sleep or do images appear? And are they hellish or heavenly? As long as we are conscious, we can't imagine the extinction of consciousness. But seeing my mother's near extinction of consciousness, I begin to see the future. Maybe we are all too convinced of our individuality. Maybe the secret is to become part of the whole.

Can an infinite higher power keep all these individual minds whirring at once? How about the minds of all the people who have ever lived? Is it possible that they are somehow all here in the ether, taking up no space but influencing us? Do ideas remain? Do memories? This is the conundrum we all face.

Watching my mother's breath moving in and out of her withered body, I try to memorize her face, her breath, her history. I breathe with her. How long will I be able to breathe with her?

"She's definitely going downhill," Ariella now says firmly. "Sometimes at night she calls out for your father."

"What does she say?"

"She calls his name."

"Does she ask him where he is?"

"No." Ariella looks at me peculiarly.

"Well, *I* would like to know where he is and what he's thinking."

She looks at me even more quizzically when I say this.

I think of my dream of my father in the snow and his anger at having to die. I remember one day about two decades ago when I called my parents one morning to check in and my mother said triumphantly, "We're still alive!" I remember the tone of amazement and victory. Then I got on with my father and he also crowed: "We're still alive!" And now he isn't and she is barely.

Will I ever get over my parents? Does anyone?

When I think of my parents crowing, "We're still alive!" I know they'll always be alive inside me.

I miss them. *Ayy yi yi* is no substitute.

I don't think I would like to end my days the way my mother is ending hers. But maybe she doesn't know she's ending her days.

How can I know how I'll feel till I get there?

There's the rub.

At home, Asher asks me how my mother is.

"Don't ask," I say.

"That bad? I hope you don't say that about me."

"But you're getting better."

"Come here," he says. I crawl into bed with him and hold him.

"I know how tough this has been for you—father, mother, me, Belinda. But I promise you I'm getting better and I will be here for you."

When he sounds strong like this, all the phantoms vanish.

But what is love? Is it giving up control?

Okay, I know it can't alter when it alteration finds. And I know that Shakespeare grokked it in the sonnet. My generation used to say "grokked" back in the day (as our kids say).

Robert Heinlein was responsible, I guess. We all read and loved his *Stranger in a Strange Land*, and after that grokked everything.

———

Back to sex. Really, folks, the search for orgasm is pure hunger. You think of it when you haven't had it in a while. After a long time you forget, become light-headed. Sexual starvation is like other forms of hunger, but hunger is not love. Of course, infants love the one who feeds them and cuddles them. But we are not infants anymore—though many people never grow up. Grown-ups, however, few as we are, know that hunger isn't love—or do we? Cats may not know, though dogs do—but let's not get into the cat or dog thing.

Before I married Asher I was, as I told you, with a young actor who was eternally hard. But was that love? I doubt it. And I doubt that even his hardness is eternal. Even *he* may get older—if he doesn't wrap himself and his old jalopy around a tree before then.

Drugs were his thing—pot, coke, meth, you name it. Who knows if he's even alive, let alone erect? When I was with him, I thought his infallible hardness had something to do with my allure. It didn't. He could get hard for anyone who petted and fed him—men, women, animal companions.

Erection—how we all seek it! The hard cock standing up and validating our existence. Men think like this—straight men and gay men both. And women do too—at least when hunger drives us. But does this hardness have anything to do with our charm and sex appeal? Who can tell?

Nikos would fuck anything. He was from Queens but loved Joyce as if he were from Killarney. We did a workshop dramatization of the last chapter of *Ulysses* together:

I was a Flower of the mountain yes when I put the rose in my hair like the Andalusian girls used to . . . and how he kissed me under the Moorish wall and I thought well as well him as another and then I asked him with my eyes to ask again yes and then he asked me would I yes to say yes my mountain flower and first I put my arms around him yes and drew him down to me so he could feel my breasts all perfume yes and his heart was going like mad and yes I said yes I will Yes.

It's become something of an old chestnut—but it works like mad. Actresses love it. The flower in the hair and all.

Even the kids love it—for the sex, I suppose. Sex is universal—like hunger. We make so much of it when we're young. We make it mean so much more than it should.

Sex is about the next generation trying to arrive. It's not about transcendentalism or philosophy or anything beyond it-self. And yet it is, too. If the gods thought it up, they were canny. It seems to mean *everything*.

When I think of all the people I married for it, all the lov-ers I chased for it . . . But it's just the gods' way of bringing us together in rare intimacy. We give it much more power than it perhaps deserves.

But you only know that when it eases its iron grip on your life.

Darling Mother,

Please don't ever die. I know you are sleepy, spend most of your time dreaming—I wish I knew your dreams—and that you can no longer speak to me or hear me. And yet I want you to live forever because I am not ready to be without a mother. Is that the most selfish of wishes? You say it is. And yet you don't want to die either. You are holding on because you fear extinction—your absolute uniqueness being lost forever. I understand that. I don't want to lose your uniqueness either, but most of all, I don't want to lose mine.

My sister Antonia phones. "I can't do this again," she explodes. "I need someone to take care of me! She lies there like a queen, but what about me! My kids don't care."

I aim for calm. I want to be calm. I want her to be calm.

"You're doing fine. This has been a really long slog. Don't give up now."

Am I saying this to her or to myself? Now, more than ever, I want peace with my sisters, no provocations, just acceptance of one another. Will we ever be able to find that?

Days go by. My mother is up and down and up and down. Sometimes I think she's dead. Sometimes I think she'll never die. Sometimes I think I am not alert enough to her new ways of communicating. When dementia has been with us a long time, the means of communicating change. Color wakes her, as does sound. Music delights her, though I think she doesn't hear. Chocolate slides on her tongue like love.

She sits up and tries to exclaim at the color of my shirt— red and purple with mossy green. An Etro confection she might have worn when she was young. Her taste in clothes was always over the top, ahead of her time, wildly artistic. But she can't speak. She croaks like a frog that might sit on a mossy green ledge, then dive swiftly into the water. She lifts her shoulders strongly, though by now she can't sit up. She exclaims without exclaiming. I know she is approving of my colorful colors—so like those she wore in her salad days. She has found a new sort of speech that is wordless. And then she begins to cough as if she will choke.

We are so unaware of different languages—not Latin and Greek, but the language of color, the language of food. We hardly know all the different kinds of human music. My mother could speak without speaking, laugh without laughing, sing without having a voice. The parents of special-needs kids know this and so do the children of the dying.

I sit by her side while she sleeps and wakes, wakes and sleeps. But one day her expression is black and blank. Something has changed. Antonia feels it and tells me she can't bear to come.

"So, don't come, I'm here," I say.

"I've been there too much," she says. "It's killing me. I'll die next. I'm dead already."

"It's okay. Don't worry."

"She can't take it," Ariella whispers. "Leave her in peace."

So I resist the temptation to call my other sister. I will stay here alone. If the hospice nurse needs to be called, we'll call her. If Mother seems to be in pain, we'll open the secret box we were told not to open. If, if, if. I can manage it. I can handle it. I'm a grown-up. I'm almost an orphan.

Her chest hardly moves. Her breathing is so light we cannot hear it. From time to time she labors to breathe and we give her decongestant. For the longest time, I wanted to be there when she passed from our planet to the moon, but now I see the passage may be imperceptible, unlike my father's. She doesn't want to stay here. She wants to join him—wherever he is. That must be love. She is dreaming of the moon.

We discuss the hospice drill, the hospice box with the doctor. We had accepted a sealed package but were told not to open it till the hospice nurse comes to the apartment.

"What's in the box?" I ask.

"The nurse will tell you when she comes," the hospice service tells me on the phone.

Over the next several hours, she has her eyes open but sees nothing. Her eyes are blank, dead letters, staring into space. Perhaps she is already on the moon.

I go home for a few hours, but when the phone shrills at six A.M., she is gone.

My sister Em and I meet in the morning darkness and go to her apartment. Toni has made it clear that she can't bear it.

"She must have passed in the wee small hours," says Ariella, with bright drops falling from her round brown eyes. She is agitated.

"Put the blanket over her head," Em says. "It's a sign of respect."

"They told me not to touch her," Ariella says. I later see she's pulled up the blanket to disguise the dead face.

I go into her room, remove the blanket, take the oxygen line out of her nose, strip the tape that holds it there, and say, "I love you, Mother." She looks like herself but very still and not yet cold. Her expression is her own.

"Don't want to go in there," Em says.

"She's still herself," I say. "She's still warm. Her face is her own. We have to say good-bye." And I take each of them by a hand and return to her bedroom. We hold hands and stare at the ancient, maternal head I've uncovered in the crypt of time.

I make myself look closely at her features—the long, aquiline nose her Japanese fans loved. The high cheekbones. The domed eyes closed. The powerful voice silenced.

"God grant me the serenity to accept the things I cannot change," my sister says.

"God gave you a good passage, thank you, God," says Ariella.

"We all love you so much," I say. "Thank you for the books, the plays, the music, the poetry, the movies. Thank you for Gershwin and Mozart and Cole Porter and Beethoven. Thank you for Duke Ellington, Gilbert and Sullivan, Mitropoulos, and Bernstein. Thank you for Yeats and Dickinson and Millay. Thank you for Leonardo and Michelangelo and Hogarth and Vigée Le Brun. Thank you for stuffing our heads full of your amazing knowledge of everything." And I kiss the air as I have kissed her before.

And we all stand stupefied by the power of death.

The hospice nurse is called but does not answer. We leave a voice-mail message saying, "We think she's gone. Please come to pronounce her." The hospice nurse never comes, never calls. Nor does the geriatric internist, who somehow knows.

As we wait together, Ariella searches her memory for all the details of the day before.

"She was sinking all day. When you came, you heard the noises she was making." Em swallows hard. I grab her hand.

Em and I had heard it differently. I heard her full lungs trying to clear. Em heard a hard coughing. Ariella heard a cracked tune. What was it?

The hospice people never came, but the funeral director did. Em didn't want to watch. Nor Ariella. I did.

They felt for a pulse. She had none. I knew that already.

They lifted her from her bed, took the sheet, and put her thin limbs into a white plastic bag, like a garment bag. I made myself watch all this to remember how little the body weighs in death. How we all shrimp away to skin and bones—even those of us who worried about our weight.

We never opened the box.

After my mother died, there were many nights when I could not sleep—though usually I sleep like the happiest of babies.

The night after she died, I paced the floor of my apartment, listening for her, and the night after we buried her, I thought of taking a sleeping pill though I never take meds except when jet lag hits. But I refrained. If my mother was around, I wanted to be there to greet her.

One night I dreamed myself in India with my husband. Each of us was sent a tantric guide, his a beautiful woman in a golden sari and mine a little Indian man who looked like Rumplestiltskin in a fairy-tale book I once had as a child. He was brown as a roasted nut and shorter than me, but he promised to give me the satisfaction I needed.

I protested that I was married and didn't want to betray my husband, but he said my husband had agreed. That night he came to me, slipped his hard, small cock into my vagina, and rambunctiously fucked me. At first I seemed to feel nothing, and then, when he withdrew with many sweet words, I felt my cunt pulsing with a fierce orgasm that even comforted me when I awoke.

The tantric sari lady brought my husband a fabulous orgasm too, and we both marveled at how long it had taken us to find this wonderful tantric island within the subcontinent. We had both found what we needed—a place where sexual satisfaction could always be found—without fear or guilt or discomfort.

"How did we miss this place?" I asked.

"We must have been nuts!" said Ash. "This is great!"

Many days later I found the morphine syringes in the box we had never opened.

The ancient Greeks knew that death is a friend. They knew that the story of Tithonus is no comedy.

The goddess of dawn, Eos, fell in love with a Trojan prince and begged Zeus to make her lover immortal. But in her mad passion she forgot to ask for his eternal youth. Tithonus became the man who could not die. He wandered the earth begging endlessly for mercy as his eyes, his limbs, his inner organs rotted and fell out and he grew more and more decrepit.

All he could do was talk, talk, talk.

Eventually he was turned into a cricket by a merciful god.

Language—the cricket has language too.

In Provence, they know the fertile wisdom of the noisy cricket.

Ash and I had a house in Provence in a lovely little village called Rousillon. The crickets make merry all night there in summer.

But death finishes nothing. Death begins the harvest—the harvest of pain, of administration, of clerical work. And the gradual transformation of a difficult parent into a demi-saint.

Scratch *demi*. Parents get nobler and nobler after they die. They also get funnier and more endearing. They come to deserve your desperate love.

15

Tender the Dead

And so I say to you, tender the dead, as you would yourself be tendered, now, in what you would describe as your life.

—Harold Pinter, *No Man's Land*

There were many times I prayed for her to die. She was so frail and so sad that I often couldn't bear to visit her. I always preferred to be with my daughter and grandson rather than with her. I did not want to stare at death until the very end. But when she finally died, my whole system went into shock. I became agitated and found it hard to sleep. One night I took a sleeping pill and found myself riding on clouds, at peace for the first time. Another night I paced the floor, unable to sleep and not wanting to take a pill. I wanted to fly with her, leaving all fear behind. I wanted to roll into her grave like some Shakespearian heroine. I wanted to scream, to cry, to exult, to dance, to die. And so the moods alternated for weeks.

There is a finality to death that cannot be anticipated by fears or prayers. When she became mute and could not stay awake for more than a few minutes at a time, I prayed for her to die. But when she died, I no longer wanted her death at all.

I found the public response to her departure quite astonishing. The response was far more than I'd thought possible

given her extreme age and how long she'd been out of the public eye. Few living people remembered her but for her children
and grandchildren. Nevertheless she was in the entertainment
wires—and once there, it seems you never die.

The trades of her time had been bought up by Fox, Thom-
son Reuters, AP, and the like. So her life was still looping
somewhere—perhaps on Mars—with *Curiosity*. Or at least
the moon.

That was gratifying to me—even though there were many
mistakes in the obit. My father was described as a vaudevillian
and so was she, though vaudeville was dead by the time they
trod the boards. My sisters got mad at me, as if I were responsible for these errors. I could not convince Em that the press
has a life of its own—often completely disconnected from history. I could not convince Antonia either. All the press stressed
the same boldface names—mine, Ash's, the artists we'd bought,
the much more famous performers my parents had worked
with. Gershwin for his apartment, Cukor for his directing,
Bibliomania for its famous autographed association copies.
The press drove me crazy, but I was used to it and didn't expect accuracy. I knew that eyeballs are driven by boldface
names, and all anyone wants today are eyeballs. Nobody cares
about truth.

But my sisters blamed me, as always.

They wanted to give away my parents' legacy—when all I
wanted was to keep it, exhibit it, make it as real as it was for
me in childhood.

"Let's meet at the apartment and discuss it," Em would say
on the telephone. "Antonia even says she'll come." And my
heart would plummet into my thousand-dollar shoes.

"Can't we do it by phone or by e-mail?" I'd plead.

"No—we all have to be there," she'd insist.

And that was how she roped me in.

There should be a name for the state of the air in an apartment when the inhabitants have gone to another circle—
purgatory, heaven, hell. It is not still, but teeming with busy
ghosts. Let's call it busy air. The Gershwins, of course, were
still there, George, Frankie, and Ira singing at their Steinways
and a gloomy cloud hanging over their heads because of the
early death of George. Everyone said the Gershwins never got
over their brother's death. I heard it from my mother—who
was great friends with Frankie Godowsky, George and Ira's
baby sister. The Gershwins were from Odessa—like my
family. They had those amazing Ashkenazic genes and could
plug songs, sing, dance, paint, write lyrics, survive Hollywood,
and transplant from Brooklyn to Manhattan without being
traumatized. Nowadays, artistic kids transplant from Manhattan to Brooklyn. In those days, they couldn't wait to leave
Brooklyn for Manhattan. But I know the backstory. Nothing
was as it seemed. Life is a dream; skimmed milk masquerades
as cream, etc.

The last time I breathed this air my mother had just
stopped breathing and the funeral parlor folk had come to
wrap her up and take her away. After that came the funeral—
like all funerals, but of course *unlike* all funerals in the vast
number of people who came—lawyers, accountants, devel-
opment directors, deranged fans with their tatty autograph
books and grubby old cameras. They gather like flies around
the dead bodies of the famous, near-famous, once-famous,
once-friends of the once-famous. Not long ago I saw them

gathering around the side door to the Carlyle on the off chance Mick Jagger might be there.

We played Gershwin throughout the funeral as my mother had once wished. Gershwin piano rolls, Gershwin's "Rhapsody in Blue," Gershwin's "An American in Paris," Gershwin's opera about Porgy and Bess. Like Gershwin, my parents were colorblind ahead of their time, and the funeral directors must have seen more people of color at my mother's funeral than they had seen at all the funerals they had organized before. We do seem to segregate our corpses. And so it was at the cemetery.

We buried her next to my father in a Jewish cemetery in Elmont, Long Island, opposite Belmont Park racetrack. The whole *mishpocheh* was there—my grandparents, Ash's grandparents, my parents and aunts and uncles and their kin, Ash's parents, aunts, and uncles, and their kin. Oddly enough, Ash's ancestors had bought plots near my ancestors—probably sold to them around the same time by some hustler/tummler from Brooklyn or the Lower East Side. First-generation Ashkenazim all had burial societies to buy land for *their* dead. Land for the dead is a Jewish tradition. We walk on the earth, then lie under it.

The thudding of earth on coffin is such a desolate sound. You suddenly realize you are *leaving* them there. How can you leave your mother in the frigid earth? And a hole opens in the heart, in the solar plexus, in the *kishkas*.

No, no, no, no, no. How can I leave my only mother there?

So we walked from grave to grave, leaving marker stones, as Jews do. We were here, we mourned, we went home. But not for long.

———

"So let's go through her things," Em said.

"Do we have to?"

"Yes, Ness," my sister said.

So we began the horrible process of combing through trash and treasures.

Em found, in a box, a pair of brass balls. They were probably Ben Wa balls. Why would my father need Ben Wa balls—for my mother? Another woman? Em took them out. They jingled as we moved them in our hands.

"Daddy's brass balls," she said. "They rightfully belong to you!"

Was it a compliment? Or an insult? I decided to take it as a compliment. One always has that choice.

"Thanks, Em," I said. "I need them. I'm happy to have them." I did not say what I thought they were. And my little sister—still five years younger and five years more innocent (though we were both hovering around sixty)—persisted in thinking they were Daddy's brass balls—which as the "boy" in the family belonged to me.

Later, at home, I felt their weight in my hands and I was sure they must have been a "naughty" gift from one of my parents' "naughty" friends. Their friends were always sending jokey sexual gifts, which, when I was an adolescent, I disdained. Open about sex and "naughtiness," my parents had arty friends like themselves who brought such gifty trinkets to their endless parties. Probably no one had ever used them as Ben Wa balls at all. At least I hoped so.

I remember once, long ago, at a party in the grand ballroom of the apartment, I spied (from the stairs) a woman friend of theirs doing a drunken striptease and singing out, "I love to drink, I love to eat, I love to fuck!"

I was utterly disgusted—as adolescents are about their parents' sexuality. Yet also fascinated. And determined to lead
my sexual life differently.

Had I? That is too deep a question for sorting treasures
and trash!

The jewelry was a different story.

Everyone wanted it. Three girls and whaddya get? A fight
over pearls?

My mother was a bohemian, a rich hippie, a girl with a
rose in her hair—but she loved jewelry. Before the seas were
dead, she and my father had played Tokyo, so there were pearls
and pearls. And such pearls as make daughters sick with
longing. Not the silly freshwater junk they pass off as pearls
now—but huge pearls, mabe pearls, matched cream-colored
pearls, pink pearls that gleamed like young nipples, baroque
pearls that glinted blue and green like cartoon aliens (the
cheap stuff), golden pearls, silvery pearls, pearly white pearls
to drape on nude breasts as if you were one of Colette's Belle
Epoque courtesans—or indeed her lover.

I had read *Chéri* and *The Last of Chéri* over and over and
dreamed of a young lover who would want to wear my pearls—
and eventually shoot himself for love of me. Though, of
course, it was not love of Léa that killed Chéri, but the im-
possibility of stopping time.

He was like me. He *was* me—but I had no gun. Gun or
no, I would accept age as Léa did and Chéri never did—and
move along the down escalator of life.

My phone pinged. It always pinged at the most inoppor-
tune times.

"Your phone," Em said.

"Fuck my phone," I said.

"No thanks," she said.

I hugged her. I was not about to tell her about the sexual fantasies my phone transmitted. My parents had been hot. How long had that lasted? A long time, I hoped. But like any daughter, I didn't want to think about it too graphically. I knew my father had frequented happy-endings massage parlors at some point in his later life. I knew because I saw his credit-card bills at that point. What else could "Asian Ending" mean? More power to him! Sex is life—but children don't want to think about their parents doing it.

We went on to the jewelry. Less confusing. Em wanted the big pink pearls. So did I.

"We should call Antonia," I said.

"She doesn't want jewelry. She only wants money," Em said.

"But she should have the chance!"

"The hell with her," Em said bitterly. "She got much more money than either of us—she had the most kids."

"I never knew it bothered you. You got the store and all the rare books."

"It was the *least* I could get since my poor dead husband rescued the business from *collapse*!"

"God, Emmy, do you *really* think that?"

"I don't think it—it's a fact. A fact is a fact is a fact. You were off making movies and getting married and married again. She was off being hysterical in Ireland and having babies! And we were *here* taking care of everyone as they deteriorated. We had no life!"

"What? You had the life you wanted—Bibliomania—the books, the autographs, the parental units that went with them. Not to mention the building on Fifty-seventh Street, appreciating in value."

"Do you realize how many mortgages it had on it? Daddy was a terrible real estate person. By the time it came to us, it had three mortgages!"

"But you sold it for a fortune!"

"A fortune?"

"Well, what *did* you sell it for?"

"Not that much," Em said.

"How much?"

"Well, if I give you the number, it'll be misleading."

"The facts, please, Em; you love facts!"

"Well, after the mortgages, the expenses of running it, the share to Mommy and Daddy, the—"

"Come on, Em, I heard you got more than a hundred million."

"That's a bald-faced lie! Who told you that?"

"I don't remember."

"But your husband is rich as Croesus, and last time I looked, you had five houses—New York, London, Paris, Aspen, Rousillon, not to mention the yacht, which is taller than most apartment buildings!"

"Have you stood it on end and measured it? You amaze me, Emmy. I never thought you were so astute at counting other people's money!"

"It was just a tiny falling-down building."

"A tiny falling-down building on Fifty-seventh Street—next to Steinway Hall!"

Em didn't answer but she looked sour. She was not happy about the way her life had worked out. That was the problem. No money could ever cure that. Money may make the world go round, but it can't cure family unhappiness. Or marital disappointment. Or the feeling you have never risked your life for joy.

I supposed she *had* got a huge amount of money for the old bookstore brownstone. I wasn't paying attention. Daddy no doubt got his share, but Em and her late husband had reaped the rest—whatever it was. Sure, there were expenses. There always were—taxes, mortgage interest, lawyers, accountants, the whole megillah. There are *always* expenses to pay, but that didn't mean she got nothing. She just wanted me to believe that, and I didn't. I felt she had stolen my patrimony in exchange for my pathetic fame, and I was mad. I was determined to have the best pearls. I should let go.

Why fight about it? I had enough. At least I thought so at the time. But I was furious. My little sister got my patrimony. It may have been a crumbling brownstone with funny-smelling stairs and more rare books than we could ever inventory correctly. It may have been so rotten as to be unrenovatable, but it had a prime location, and my parents had bought it in 1951! It was the way of my family to always poor-mouth their real estate, to complain about their investments, in order to undo the evil eye of envy. But if you figured that they had started buying rare books and autographs before anyone knew what they were worth, that all their real estate was in areas that went up, up, up, that they had terrific taste and knew all the actors, artists, and composers of their time— you knew that whoever got their stuff would make out like a bandit.

I wanted the pink pearls, goddamnit! And I was gonna have them—as well as my brass balls!

We looked for the pearls. Mother used to keep them in a

locked box built into the floor of her bedroom under the mauve Chinese rug.

We searched for the key for hours, found it in a jewelry box in Mother's dressing room, and with held breath opened the floor safe. It was full of those little silk bags and boxes Japanese jewelers used to display the pearls in, but not a necklace was left. There were a few loose pearls—scratched and mismatched—but no necklaces, no rings, no pins, no earrings.

"Where have they gone?" Em wailed.

"Where does anything go?" I said. "Pearls are live substances. They rolled away."

"*You* took them!" Em said.

"I wish I had, but I didn't."

Em glared at me the way a pawnbroker looks at a bad risk. "Tell me the truth."

"I always tell you the truth," I said. "And you always think I'm lying."

"Who the hell took them?"

"Anyone could have—a caregiver, a nurse, a cook. Mother had so many people in and out of her life. This happens all the time. 'Nothing in the safe but a rubber mouse,' my friend Livia told me after her mother died. 'Her huge canary diamond replaced with glass,' Clarissa said. Happens all the time. Jewels walk away and their gleam was all in your mind. Maybe they never existed—like the diamond as big as the Ritz or the jeweled forests of the twelve dancing sisters."

"Goddamnit!" Em said. "She should have given them to us years ago!"

"I guess," I said. But secretly I was exultant. Em would not get them. No one would.

"You can be philosophical—with all the jewelry Asher gave you!"

"Do you want it? Wanna trade it for your First Folio?"

Em looked at me cynically. "Sold it ages ago," she crowed.

"Let's not do this anymore," I said. "I'm exhausted." Why was I fighting about money and jewelry with someone I deeply loved? I wanted to take it all back. Probably she did too.

"Me too," said Em.

And we locked the empty safe, unrolled the carpet, and left by the front door. One of these days I would have to find forgiveness for and with my sisters. It was my next life challenge.

After we buried my mother, I could not believe she was dead. I'd wake up every morning with a vision of her lying in bed as usual on the other side of the park.

"I must go see her!" I'd admonish myself. And then I'd remember that what was left of her was in the cemetery. But my memories of her changed. Instead of the ghostly centurion lying in bed, she became the energetic mother of my youth. She was ice-skating, dancing, jumping, shouting, full of beans. Though I could not go back in time, it seemed she could. That was the secret to going back in time: You had to be dead to do it.

I felt as if someone had knocked all the foundations out from under me, as if I were floating in space with no Earth to land on. Then I would go to Glinda's house and stare at the sleeping form of my grandson, Leo. Now he was the one who grounded me. He was my rock—small as he was.

We are held to this life by our connections with others—family, friends, lovers. Otherwise we might drift off in space. I wished for Isadora to be there with me, but she had taken off on a long trip to India.

The next time I went to my parents' apartment, I found myself in the midst of a play. The place was filled with movers, boxes, relatives sorting through old photographs, junk dealers, Realtors, painters, floor scrapers, and curiosity seekers. I never thought we'd sell the family dump, but it was too valuable to keep and the money glistened just out of sight. My parents had once rented it for two hundred dollars a month and now it was worth millions. So we had to get rid of tons and tons of stuff—nobody had room to keep it. The photographs were the worst, the trivia of lost lives.

What I really wanted to do was to create a museum for my parents—with walls of photographs, all the portraits of them and their children—us!—a museum that could never be destroyed. And the place for it was obvious: the old Bibliomania brownstone with its strange smells and stained walls. But my sister had sold it. And now we were preparing to sell the apartment. My parents would be reduced to their narrow graves, their last real estate. No museum of innocence or experience would ever hold their memories. Everything would be sold for lack of space. Memories giving way to money.

I wish I believed in God—any god really. Lakshmi, Ganesha, Jesus, Allah. I wish I believed my mother was not just rotting in her coffin in the ground. I wish I believed her life meant something besides giving birth to me and my sisters. I wish there was a golden abacus totting up her worth in heaven or an angelic ascension or transformation into sainthood—something to make her life have meaning as she left it, something besides her fleeting fame and aging children. Why can't I believe in a god or goddess or grace? Why does her life become a heap of dust—and by extension mine? All her joie de vivre, her rage, her talent now rotting in a box. The Italian proverb goes: "After the game, both king and pawn lie in the same box."

The queen and pawn too. I wish I believed that transfiguration followed death. I wish I believed.

But of course the Buddha believed in neither birth nor death. When the right conditions are present, the being manifests itself. When they are not present, the being remains hidden. My mother was hidden now. Perhaps she would manifest again in another form. She herself had always believed that. She adored flowers and fruits and vegetables and would not have minded being born again as a dahlia, a rose, or a peony. Even a peach. Or a tomato. She knew that everything was connected.

Was that comforting? Yes and no. Birth and death are meaningless concepts in Buddhism. The wave rises to a crest, flows along, then breaks and rises again. We are waves that will rise again, fall again, rise again. We are not solid but fluid. We love the sea because we *are* the sea. A wave is a wave is a wave. Apologies to Gertrude Stein.

I had sent Isadora's pages to my agent and she had gone crazy over them. I knew I was not authorized to share them, so I told the agent that they were written by a friend called Will Wilde. Where I got the name, I cannot tell you. Will for Shakespeare? Wilde for Oscar? Two favorite writers of mine. But who cares? The names matter less than the vision.

My agent sold her book to a movie company for a shitload of money and then it was sold to a publishing company for another shitload.

I got really nervous about telling Isadora. I'd had no right to do this and now it appeared that Will Wilde was about to become a star.

Alone on his asteroid, Will Wilde was preparing for his debut. What the fuck would I do?

PART IV

Summer

16

Bollywood in Goa

For they had lived together long enough to know
that love was always love, anytime and anyplace,
but it was more solid the closer it came to death.

—Gabriel García Márquez,
Love in the Time of Cholera

The most important thing to remember is that life is a comedy. Here I had lost my father, my mother, my dog, and almost my husband, but I was still able to see the absurdity of life. And that was when I received the invitation to India. This was wonderful since we had been planning a trip to India anyway.

Never die without seeing India. Luck was with us because just as we had decided to flee New York for the gorgeous and terrifying subcontinent, a film festival in Goa invited me to participate. It seemed that my hoary old soap, *Blair's World*, had become a huge hit in India. I had almost forgotten it as millions of Indians were watching it and identifying with it.

The most curious thing about our world of indelible media is how far it travels and how lasting it is. Somewhere in another galaxy, aliens are watching *I Love Lucy* and trying to understand what it all means. I can imagine a day when the earth has become uninhabitable but our soap operas are streaming in space. Is this what immortality means?

I had been to India before but Ash had not. Anyway, India is so amazingly diverse and huge that you can hardly know it at all without a thousand trips. You have to live there to even begin to appreciate its aromas and its astonishing diversity. India is a vast cosmos full of colors and smells and wonders and horrors. I had visited Mumbai, New Delhi, and Rajasthan and I knew I had only scratched the surface of the subcontinent. Of course, I was deeply cynical about the possibility of India transforming my life. I hardly believed such things were possible. But I needed a break from all the deaths that had consumed me—and India seemed like the place to go. I had recently read a hilarious and moving book set partly in Varanasi and I thought it evoked the ferocious contrasts of India—spirituality and sewage, holiness and humbug, high civilization and low comedy. I knew Asher and I had to go to India together, but I didn't yet know why. In my adolescence I had read Rabindranath Tagore and swooned. Later I fell in love with India according to Merchant Ivory. Still later I read E. M. Forster's *A Passage to India* relentlessly, musing on which of the characters might have been inspired by his Indian lover. I knew none of these Indias—nor indeed Hermann Hesse's nor Salman Rushdie's nor Kiran Desai's—was the real India. Possibly there was no real India any more than there is a real America. Still, I had to go again. Venice was once the place where Americans and Europeans found a treasure palace of the body and the spirit in the nineteenth century. In the twenty-first century, it is India. We conjure it as an ideal place—projecting our need onto an imaginary India. I was no different than any other deluded dreamer.

We took off for Dubai on Ali Baba Airlines—with its private roomettes, showers, and rose-scented boudoirs. Ali Baba makes other airlines seem like cattle transport. Flight attendants are forever bringing you hot towels—which really are towels and really are hot—and silk pajamas and embroidered slippers. Little plates of delicacies are available whether you are Muslim, Hindu, Jewish, or none of the above. No forbidden foods are even seen or tasted. How the staff kept all this straight was amazing. But they did. We flew and flew and flew until we flew deep into the mythic past. And mythic present.

Goa was a Portuguese colony till the sixties—incredibly enough. Goa has gorgeous cathedrals, public squares that seem positively European, and the memories of its own Inquisition. Its history is endlessly fascinating.

The airport was typical Indian chaos. If you put down your bag or your cell phone, it will be stolen faster than you can say "maharishi." You see Sikhs in turbans, Arabs in long white desert garb, women in burkas or blue jeans. The whole diversity of the world can be seen at an Indian airport. We looked around for some sign of our sponsors—Bollywood in Goa—and finally saw a sign proclaiming "Ms. Blair and guest."

I presumed the waving, cheering contingent was for me. We had an entourage of five: a willowy young woman named Parvati wearing a cream and gold sari; her porter in a gold turban; and three other turbaned gentlemen from the conference whose roles were not immediately clear. They took our hand luggage and accompanied us to a car.

"I am your shadow for the conference," Parvati said. "I am to take you everywhere and facilitate for you. Don't worry about your other bags. My colleagues will fetch them and bring them to your hotel."

She took my baggage receipts from me and sent the three gentlemen away with a wave of her hand.

"We'll never see our luggage again," I said to Asher with my typical anxiety.

"So we'll buy new things," he said. "Don't worry." India had already made Asher calm. But it wasn't only India—it was having survived his near-death crisis. And I had survived it too. If meditation is looking for the light in yourself, I had glimpsed the light. I had needed sex so much I didn't realize it was different from love.

It may be the climate, the damp, the riot of colors—or indeed it may be jet lag—but like nearly dying, India makes you feel different about your life. It's like a rebirth. There you are in the cradle of religion and ancient civilization and you feel the possibility of starting your life anew.

It's true that the quest for enlightenment seems hard-wired into the human psyche. Each civilization has conceived of this journey differently—and in our time the journey to India has held a special place in the human heart. It's where you learn who you are and what you believe. It's foreign and exotic enough to play the role Italy played for eighteenth-century connoisseurs. I have so many friends who have gone to India to change their lives, and most of them claimed that it did. India is a simmering pot of mythologies and mysteries. India is a touchstone more than a tourist destination.

When we got to our suite, we discovered rose petals strewn on our immense gold silk coverlet and two handsome young turbaned butlers ready to unpack our bags in a dressing room with a marble pool. Asher shooed them away with wads of rupees and collapsed, as did I, on the bed. We both slept for who knows how long. In my dreams I began to segue in and out of different phases of my life—time traveling again as if India were a wormhole into the past. My dreams were so vivid that they hardly felt dreamlike. Right before I awoke, I had one of my dreams of cocks—pink cocks, brown cocks, yellow cocks—all hard and ready to fuck me. Then Asher awoke and really did make love to me slowly. My dream had changed him, made him sensitive in a new way. We melded into each other like two parts of one person. I hadn't understood that before but now I did. We had never before taken the time for slow sex in a fast world. I remembered Isadora's phrase—"slow sex in a fast world."

Or maybe it was India. His sexuality had returned. Or possibly we both had become young again, as I had wished, or possibly it was the first time I was giving up control. If ecstasy exists anywhere, it surely exists in India. Maybe I was experiencing for the first time what Isadora had talked about. Was this surrender?

"Ness, Ness, Ness," Asher chanted, driving himself into my wet center. We rose after that and bathed in the marble pool. Sitting in the warm water filled with rose petals, I felt like I was reliving the first weekend we spent together in my hot tub in Vermont. We had spent hours communing, telling each other the stories of our lives. Time was abolished between us—as it was when first we met. I remembered all the reasons I loved him, and he could feel it. It was as if we had entered a new level of understanding.

"Nobody ever really knew me before I met you," Asher said.

"Me you too," I said. "And I want to be known by you, wholeheartedly."

"Or wholecuntedly," he said. "Is that a word?"

"It is now," I said.

Jet-lagged as we were, we were invited to appear at a grand party on the seashore given by one of the sponsors of the conference—a cell phone mogul with more money than taste. His house was a white marble pavilion fashioned as a smaller copy of the Taj Mahal in Agra. His wife was in white, he was in white, and his footmen and waiters wore crimson kurtas. The food was a mélange of western and Indian dishes set out on mirrored trays.

"You were brilliant as Blair," he told me. "Scheming, conniving, and hypocritical, just like most beautiful women. Are you also like that in your life?"

"I hope not," I said. "She's meant to be a villainess, not an angel."

"Well—Indian women love you and also Indian men—we are all at your feet. We think you no less than a manifestation of Kali."

"Shall I feel complimented?"

"Without a doubt, my dear lady. Being evil is so much more dramatic than being good."

At that point, his wife rushed up, grabbed my hand, and kissed it passionately. "You have revealed the soul of womanhood," she blathered. "You have released the drama of the female soul."

I wasn't sure how to respond but remembered that "Thank you" is an all-purpose salve.

"Thank you, thank you," I told my hostess. "How very kind of you to invite me."

"And you may notice that your episodes are playing in a continuous loop throughout the party." She pointed to a huge screen on the far wall—and there I was as Blair, twenty years younger and wearing huge shoulder pads. It was odd to see myself somehow—like going into a time warp and becoming young again. Once, I had wanted nothing more. Now that it had come true, I wondered what the dues would be.

"I do feel young again," I said to my new friends.

"And still as beautiful," said Ash.

Our hostess commanded food be brought for us on mirrored trays, and she and her husband accompanied us to a nearby table where the four of us might sit.

"You know, of course, that all of India thinks you a goddess," our hostess said.

"But you have so many more wonderful goddesses," I said.

"Ah, but we worship images," our hostess said, "flickering images from the West."

"That is exactly our problem," said her husband. "We have turned our faces to the West when India is the mother of us all. We must learn to worship her again."

"I couldn't agree more. I would do anything to be an Indian goddess—or even to play one."

"So you will stay and make a movie here?" our host proposed.

"Why not?"

"My dream is to reawaken the female soul of India with my movie about Indian goddesses. Then you will you read my script?"

"With pleasure," I said carelessly. "As soon as I get over my jet lag."

"Splendid!" said the mogul, whose name, it turned out,

was Rajeev. His wife was jubilant at my answer. I was used to promises at parties that were never kept. How was I to know if there really was a script? Indians are exuberant and full of hyperbole—like the colors of their gorgeous land. They may flatter you one moment and completely forget you the next. They love the aura of fame—no matter how tarnished. They are fame-cravers as much as Americans and Brits are.

Which is why it didn't surprise me that Nigel Cavendish and his Vivienne were also at the party. Vivienne was perhaps twenty-five and heavily pregnant. Nigel and I greeted each other like old mates and introduced our spouses to each other.

"Why are *you* here?" I asked Nigel.

"I've become madly famous in India," Nigel said, "so Bollywood called. I'm doing a movie here."

"How delightful! Break a leg! You know I wish you great success."

"And I you—always," said Nigel.

There was no longer any electricity between us, and our partners knew it.

Asher reached out and shook Nigel's hand and Vivienne and I gave each other fake kisses on both cheeks.

Well, Nigel and I had been faithful in our fashion. As Cole Porter wrote, "I'm always true to you, darlin' in my fashion. . . ."

So there I was like Nigel—forgotten in my own country but famous in Asia. How strange it was to be famous again. Walking through the hotel lobby, I'd be accosted by gushing fans telling me how Blair had changed their lives. It was astonishing. I had wished to be young again, and somehow by coming to India I was.

Yet I was an orphan now. When your parents live as long

as mine had, you think they are never going to die. I had not processed either death. I had run away instead. My father and mother haunted me. They were constantly talking to me, telling me not to forget them.

I've always believed that ancestor worship is the oldest religion. Parental voices in our heads are the strongest prayers. The dead live within us. We keep them alive. They never die.

Tourists usually visit Goa for the beaches, but there are ancient caves in the vicinity—perhaps not as famous as Ellora or Elephanta, but even older and more mysterious. I had read about Avalem and Khandepar and was eager to visit. Ash was tired and jet-lagged and not so sure, but when he had rested for a few days, I convinced my shadow, Parvati, to take us there.

She hesitated, said we must purify ourselves first, that the caves were a test for the imagination, that they were not easy to visit. She was clearly discouraging me—which only made me more curious. Eventually, I had to agree to do yoga and cleansings with her for a week before she consented to take us.

"These caves are more than a tourist destination," she told me. "They are sacred and dangerous, and many travelers have never returned. You will only return if you have the proper humility. Once you get there it will be too late to purify yourself or to depart if the god commands you to stay. You must have respect and calmness. You must agree to have forgiven all your enemies."

"What difference does that make?" I asked.

"All the difference in the world," Parvati said. "People who are full of rage never appear again aboveground."

———

It is always harder to get to places in India than you antici-
pate. The roads are bad, the weather unpredictable, and you
may be constantly waylaid by beggars, animals, traffic jams,
buses full of tourists, and herds of cattle. What happens on
the way from here to there cannot even be called traffic. It's
more like a hurricane hitting Noah's ark. We traveled in a
rundown Volkswagen buslet begrimed with the dust of the
road, decorated with silken banners, driven by a chauffeur and
a navigator who argued about the route.

After what seemed like several hours, we arrived at a rock-
cut temple guarded by a huge gargoyle. We seemed to be the
only tourists.

The driver and navigator offered us water, face wipes, and
snacks but declared that they would rather wait outside than
enter the caves. They were reputed to be dangerous, possibly
haunted, and full of unmarked turnings. There was also a hidden lake where, it was said, tourists had drowned. Oh no—
they were not going in with us—never mind the rupees.

As Parvati, Ash, and I walked in, the first object we saw
was a huge lingam stone—the tireless penis of Krishna, with
which he had fecundated the world and all its beings. We
heard the sounds of running water, felt the dampness to our
very bones, and soon came into a chamber where the life of a
human being was told in monumental statues: the little boy,
the adolescent, the bridegroom with his beautiful melon-
breasted bride, the father surrounded by children, the mother
with her children worshipping her and kissing the hem of her
garment, the old father as a sadhu with his ash-covered limbs
and his begging bowl. As we wandered past these statues in

the gloom, the cave became colder and colder and we began to shiver.

"We can go back," Parvati said. "We can cut our visit short." Her words only made me want to stay.

We climbed down and down on slippery stone where we nearly lost our footing. Was it the face of my friend Isadora I saw peering out of the mouth of a cave? Well then, everything would be all right. She would forgive me for selling her out as Will Wilde. She would laugh that I had not asked her permission. After all, there was no way she would have sent the manuscript out herself. I knew that and she knew that. Had I asked her, she would have found some way not to answer. I knew Isadora. Like all real writers, she had no faith in what she had written. Only amateurs think their writing is perfect. Was it Thomas Mann who said, "A writer is someone for whom writing is more difficult than it is for other people"? I knew that Isadora wanted to be read as we all want to be read. Words can defeat death. Most books turn to dust, like most people. But a few of them remain—sometimes only in fragments like the books of Sappho. Never mind. Even those fragments can fly.

I stared toward the wet wall where statues of the gods were roughly carved in bas-relief. Suddenly, a flash of light. The faces of the gods became the faces of our parents. Then the light went dead. Was I dreaming or imagining? The statues of the god were gone—and with them the faces of our parents.

Do not cry for us, for we have had our lives, I thought I heard my father say before his stone face turned back into the face of the god.

You must now seize your life, I heard my mother whisper.

Don't be afraid. Fear is a waste of life. Her stone face now soft-ened into the goddess's face.

Deeper into the cave we walked, following the sound of rushing water. We came upon a steaming lake where an in-finity of gods and goddesses jumped up above the surface of the water for an instant and then submerged and dissolved as if they'd never been.

"It is said that in this cave we all see only what we're meant to see," Parvati said.

"And what do you see?" I asked her.

"I see myself as a slave of the god, left upon the temple steps, to become the concubine of princes. My family was un-touchable once. I weep for the infant I was."

"I cannot see any infants at all," I said.

"Of course not. You only see what you are meant to see."

We descended deeper and deeper into the earth.

Ash ran ahead and embraced a standing rock, weeping.

"Who is that?" I asked.

"I think it is my father," Ash said. "Shall I forgive him, or myself?" Ash had always hated his father. I looked at Asher's face in the darkness and hugged him very tight.

But all I saw was a man-size tower of rock, bathed in water flowing over stone.

"Without forgiveness, we are lost," I said.

"There are many levels of civilization in this cave," Parvati said. "No one agrees on its origins, nor has it ever been mapped. I think we should turn back."

I looked behind me—mist before a wall of rock. Ahead of me were steps leading farther down.

"But where to turn?" I asked.

Panic seized me. We would never get out. The driver and

his navigator had been right. There was no way out of this un-mapped cave.

"Some people say the origin of this cave is Buddhist and that the only way to emerge from it is to still the chatter in your mind. As long as fear commands you, you'll be trapped here forever." Who said that? Was it Parvati, or the god in the cave? Impossible to know.

We began to breathe in unison. Parvati counted our breaths in the echoing chamber. She went on and on until it seemed she had been counting forever. There is a pause at the end of each breath where it is said you may decide which world to enter. I considered death, but I chose life.

How much I missed my mother! Not the mother she had be-come at the end of her life, but the vibrant young woman who took us flying to Catalina when we were little girls. The vision of Santa Catalina took me back, back, back to my mother lacing up our sneakers and laughing when we were afraid to venture into the plane. She was so beautiful and young and exuberant. I couldn't imagine life without her!

All the tears that refused to flow at her funeral, at her burial, now flowed down my cheeks, immersing me as if with the amniotic fluid that had sustained me inside her for nine months. I was soaked with tears. Their glistening illuminated the path upward, the steps that led out of the cave.

As we were making our way back to the hotel, we all were very silent.

"I never expected to see my father again," Ash said. "Who knew he was in India—in a cave! I have to forgive him so I can forgive myself."

———

We come to India because India is the past of the human race. We burrow in her caves as in the innards of our mothers. We search for meaning in these amazing wombs of time. Once I dreamed of reliving my youth through magic. Now I understand that I relive my youth every day of my life. As a mother, as a grandmother, as a wife, I am in the past, the present, the future all at once. That is the gift that India gives. India has the gift of abolishing time.

As we were driving back to Goa in the gathering darkness, Parvati said, "India has ignited your heart—as Tagore predicted. I have seen Americans transformed this way many times. It is not only the descent into the caves, but the ability to suddenly look at your life differently."

"But why?" I asked.

"There is no answer to that," she said. "Unless the answer is karma."

"But what is karma?" I asked.

"Some translate it as fate," she said. "To me it is more than that. I think of it as all the influences of your acts stored up in your many lifetimes. Hopefully you will earn the gift of total extinction—never having to be born again in any form. You Westerners dream of immortality while we dream of its opposite."

"So you would like to grow enlightened enough not to have to live again?"

"That's the idea," Parvati said.

"So life is not the ultimate blessing?" I asked.

"Far from it," she said.

"We don't think of not being born again as extinction, but as union with our creator."

"If I think of it that way, it's another story," I said. "I can hardly wrap my head around it."

"It's not easy," Parvati said. "But if you think that all the actions of each of your many lives can prepare you for reunion with the divine or not, then it makes more sense. You were born from the godhead and will return there—it's only a question of how long it takes." Then Parvati recited parts of a poem by Tagore that went like this:

"Go not to the temple to put flowers upon the feet of God,
First fill your own house with the fragrance of Love . . .

Go not to the temple to pray on bended knees,
First bend down to lift someone who is downtrodden.

Go not to the temple to ask for forgiveness for your sins,
First forgive from your heart those who have sinned against you."

"What does that mean?" Ash asked. "Why would I want to be reunited with a god?"

"To find Nirvana," Parvati said. "And forgiveness is the only key to Nirvana. You forgive your enemies and then the gods forgive you. That way, you never have to be born again."

Later, when Ash and I were alone in our hotel room, he said, "All these caves are like gigantic earthworks. They make me understand what I was aiming at. I was drawn to earth art because somehow I knew it was the most ancient art of all. Burrowing into the earth is like burrowing back into your mother so you can be born again. I don't buy this whole lust for annihilation."

"It's all about the fear of dying," I said. "We just keep making up different philosophies to deal with our fear. And it's all so ridiculous because once we are dead we are utterly fearless. Death is fearlessness. It's the anticipation of our dying that's the problem."

"When we were in the cave, I suddenly realized why I had such a fierce drive to get rich when I was younger."

"Why?"

"I thought that wealth would protect me from dying. And for a long time, even after I met you, I thought I was protected. But after my aneurysm, I discovered that I am not immune to the fate of others. My sense of specialness was lifted."

"So are you more afraid now—of dying?"

"Oddly, I am less afraid. I think of the millions and millions of people who have been through that passage without difficulty, and I am more curious about it than I am afraid. Maybe I have lived many times before and maybe I will live again."

"But I thought you said you couldn't believe in reincarnation?"

"I never said that."

"I thought you did."

"No—I think reincarnation would be terrific—as long as I was reincarnated with you."

Ash and I had broken some barrier—as if India were a kind

of second honeymoon for us. Come to think of it, we'd never had a first honeymoon. We'd just plunged into our life together—our schedule dictated by Glinda's school schedule. But now we were alone together and we found we really loved each other. When I was with Ash, I was never lonely. That was what sex with strangers promised but could not deliver. I now thought I must have been crazy to seek intimacy there.

That night there was a huge party on the grounds of the hotel and in the adjoining ballrooms. You could tell who the sponsors were—Coca-Cola and Chivas Regal—because they'd set up enormous chaser lights over the outdoor bars.

I found that I could hardly walk across the garden without some beautiful older woman in a glorious sari grabbing me around the waist and telling me that Blair had changed her life. This was perplexing to me.

"Why?" I asked.

"Because she gave us permission to be tough yet feminine," one older actress called Rhadka explained. "Indian women needed that permission."

"But your goddesses are strong yet feminine. Isn't that enough?"

"We tend to ignore our goddesses," she said. "But your television goddesses give us permission to be ourselves. And for that we must thank you."

"But why do women always need permission to be ourselves?" My question lingered in the air unanswered.

When it was time for me to give my presentation, I used this as my opener: "Why do we as women need permission to be ourselves? So many people have thanked me for giving them permission to be real, to be honest—but why do we need this permission? Who took away our self-given permission, and why? I think if we could answer this question, we'd be well on the way to improving women's lives all over the globe. So let me just say—we have our own permission. And that ought to be quite enough for us!"

If Blair had galvanized the women, the notion of giving ourselves permission energized them even more. As I walked through the garden, women reached out to touch me. The need for self-affirmation was so great.

"Will you be my guru?" one beautiful young actress asked me.

"I am trying to tell you that you are already your own guru," I said. "You *are* strong and powerful. You only have to know how powerful and full of life you are!"

And then, as if by an act of the gods—the lights went out.

Hundreds of people in the ballroom and garden, wandering in the dark. Waiters brought candles and flashlights. Food continued to be served. But suddenly we were back in the ancient era of caves. The music went on playing.

In the darkness, I was embraced again and again by people I could not see. I could feel their warmth, hear the music, smell their perfume. I thought of the strangeness of life, how it continues even in darkness. The past was unknown and so was the future. We might as well be living in that cave where all the statues become our parents and we fear we will never escape. We are here in the darkness hoping to be born again. That is why we have come to the place where civilization was created again and again.

"When once I leave this body, shall I come back to the world?" Tagore asked. Do we ever know?

I looked around for Asher, but could not see him in the darkness. All I saw were the moving shadows that might as well have been shades of the dead. I had the feeling we had never emerged from the cave, that we were stuck there forever because of our lack of humility, our lack of faith.

I realized that all my life I had substituted cynicism for faith. I had protected myself from deep knowledge of myself. Now I made a promise to the gods—to myself—to shed that cynical skin and explore forgiveness, humility, love.

How little I knew myself until I descended into the earth in search of my ancestors. How little I knew of those I claimed to love!

Without seeing where I was going, I walked and walked over the wet grass until I found the waves lapping at my feet. I saw the statues of my parents in my mind's eye. I felt a powerful embrace in the darkness. And when I turned to look, I saw Asher.

"We have so many mysteries to solve," he said.

"Perhaps we will solve them together in our next life," I said.

"As long as we are together, we can do it," Ash said, the water lapping over our toes as if to whisper its assent.

ACKNOWLEDGMENTS

Thanks to:

Ken Burrows and Gerri Karetsky, who kept saying, "You always say that," when I despaired that I could not write this book.

Ann Pinkerton and Clarice Kestenbaum, who knew I could write even when I forgot.

Elizabeth Sheinkman and Adrienne Brodeur, who read this novel before it was ready and always believed in it.

Jennifer Enderlin, who showed me that great editing is still alive and well in the publishing world.

Dr. Harold Koplewicz, who kept saying my title had to be *Fear of Dying*, even before I was able to appreciate it (my original working title was *Happily Married Woman*).

When I'm working on a book, I'm always terrified of showing it for fear that the magic will evaporate. I now recommend this to all my writing students. Vladimir Nabokov says somewhere that he wrote an early short story about his passion for a very young girl and it took decades for it to turn into *Lolita*. It needed to grow "the wings and the claws of a novel." I have learned that novels take as long as they take.